THE CHESSMEN THIEF

BARBARA HENDERSON

pokey hat

First published in 2021 by Pokey Hat

Pokey Hat is an imprint of Cranachan Publishing Limited

ISBN: 978-1-911279-85-3

eISBN: 978-1-911279-86-0

www.cranachanpublishing.co.uk

@cranachanbooks

cranachan

For Papa, my father, who loved to play chess.

For Papa, my father, who loved to play chess.

1

THE BROKEN TUSK

I stagger under the weight of the tusks, more than half my height: long, heavy, dense and slippery, all at the same time.

'In here!' Master Gunnar waves his arms impatiently, the saw already in his hand. I shouldn't have attempted to carry two at once. Entering the workshop, the tip of one catches the wooden doorframe, the other gets tangled in the leather hide which hangs in front to keep the worst of the wind out… and I'm done for!

If I was to slow time down, it happens like this: the first walrus tusk slides from my grasp, the bent tip catches my chin, slashing a scratch across it and forcing my face sideways. It startles me enough to drop the other tusk, which bounces off my chest, crashing onto my legs before clattering to the stone floor. The sound. It's the sound that's worst of all. It's a splinter and a crack and a crunch, and I am already ducking. Too late. Master

Gunnar roars his anger and casts aside his saw. His huge, pockmarked fist flies towards my face.

I crumple under the impact. Trying to rise from the splinter-strewn flagstones of the workshop, I lift my head, but everything spins, and I fall to the floor once more.

'Get up, thrall!'

He is not finished with me. Grasping me by the back of my garment he pulls my slight body to its feet. I raise my arms to protect my face and he hesitates, his curled hand hovering in the air like Thor's hammer. It gives me time.

'I've never dropped a tusk before, Master Gunnar! Never once have I broken a tusk.' I rush the words out in my defence.

It's true. I carry the heavy walrus tusks in from the trading post by the harbour, all the way up to the workshop on top of this hill where the light lingers longest, affording the craftsmen a longer workday. But today, my forehead burns with fever, my throat retches up the meagre slave-rations I am given, and shivers would shake the whole of me if I let them. Master Gunnar won't want to hear any of that.

I prepare for another blow, but he spins instead towards his fellow craftsmen who have gathered round by now. There is anguished discussion in Norse. I stoop out of the way and swiftly retreat into my corner where

I touch my burst lip. I cup some water from the bucket they use to wash away the carving dust in my hands and sip. It's wet, and that's all that matters.

'The Scots make for the worst slaves', Old Erik mutters and wanders back to his workbench. Despite what he says, he is kind, kinder than the rest. He doesn't want to see me beaten any more.

Crouching in the straw, I cling to the hazy memories of a home I barely remember. An island off the western coast of Scotland. How long has it been? Four winters already? I try to mark the sun-downs on a beam above the workshop corner where I sleep, but it's so damaged and slashed that I don't know which marks are mine anymore. Did another thrall before me do the same? Where was he taken from if he did? England, Scotland, Ireland, Saxony? At least I haven't forgotten where I came from, or the words of my people, even if I recite them only to myself at night. Without Mother, there is no one to speak the Gaelic to anymore. In any case, Norse is my heart language now.

Gunnar approaches and I resume my defence. 'I am sorry. I… I wanted to be strong and find favour.' I feel myself dragged back to the doorway. Through it, I can see into the courtyard where the dawn mists hang like strips of dried fish. They want me there while they inspect the damage.

The craftsmen are bent over the remains of the broken

tusk, bemoaning what's left of the priceless material. The other tusk looks intact from here. It could have been worse. I wipe my face on the side of my tunic as loud volleys of outrage pass over me.

'I'll be more careful. I will not carry more than one,' I mumble.

Gunnar leans over to me. 'You don't get it, do you? Do you never listen?'

'I know walrus ivory is expensive.'

'That's not what I mean, thrall! We are working on—'

But I never find out what it is that he was going to tell me because the sound of horses' whinnying is carried on the wind and hoofbeats ring out nearby.

2

THE ARCHBISHOP'S VISIT

His face drops. 'Begone!' Gunnar hisses when he takes another look at me—I must look a sight by now. I retreat back to the workshop corner where a pile of straw and a rough, flat wad of wool are the only sign of my occupancy, there the light is low. But over by the windows, which face out west towards the sea, the craftsmen work, squinting, cutting, filing and honing wood, whale teeth and walrus ivory into something even more precious. Treasures.

The horses have arrived and I hear the voices of several men, one with long words, weighted with wisdom. It is a deep voice and I trust it, despite all its learning and complicated talk. 'We'll speak inside,' the voice commands gently.

'Of course, Archbishop.' Gunnar's voice drips with honey now and I self-consciously touch my swollen lip. He directs the visitors in and I see their feet as they walk by, shod with leather in the fashion of the rich. How I'd love to see the new Archbishop, Jon Birgersson. I have heard much about this learned man, respected by all, although people say his right-hand man looks like a devil in church attire. I am supposed to stay out of sight, but what is the harm in a little peek?

'Listen, craftsman. As I said in my earlier message, I need you to fashion me some gifts for the leaders of the lands I'll visit. Perhaps something like this.' The Archbishop taps his beautifully decorated, curled staff, the symbol of his office. 'As you know, mine is a new Archdiocese which includes Shetland, Orkney and the Southern Isles. We sail after the turn of the moon. You must make haste. I have a design in mind.'

He describes the interwoven patterns, the heraldic animals and symbols of our Christian faith to be carved into the ivory to create a crozier hook, to top a bishop's staff. A symbol to unite the churches under this man's governance.

Gunnar, however, looks at the ground. 'Erm, Archbishop, there is just one problem. Our raw materials. We are waiting for another delivery of walrus tusks, and, you see, we…'

The Archbishop taps his foot, but that is all I can see.

'We, erm, may not have pieces big enough to make croziers. In fact, we have broken bits and offcuts, but only one complete tusk.'

There is a silence which is much worse than an

exclamation. It washes in and out of the workshop like the ebb and flow of the sea with each wave. Finally, the Archbishop speaks. 'What gift could I possibly bestow, made of smashed rubble? I was informed that this workshop is renowned for being the best in all of Trondheim. All of the Norse lands, in fact.'

Einar steps forward. 'And we are the best, Archbishop.'

I imagine the glint in the craftsman's eye as he thinks of the handsome payment. But the visitors already gather their garments and turn. The Archbishop's advisor scoffs. 'You can't even make a chalice out of such small pieces. What sort of gift could be fashioned from fragments and be fit for this Archbishop, Jon Birgersson, our greatest church father? No, we will have to take our business elsewhere.'

Old Erik's workbench stands nearest to my corner and a thought strikes me. *Maybe, maybe not all is lost.*

'Game pieces,' I whisper to the old man, and his eyebrows shoot up. 'Hnefatafl. Or even chess pieces,' I add.

My work is done. The old craftsman clears his throat. 'Honoured Archbishop, pardon me, but have you considered… have you considered making a gift of gaming sets? Gaming pieces can be made to look impressive and can be easily carved from fragments like these.'

The Archbishop sighs, but somehow there is kindness

in the sigh. 'Make me an example and I shall think on it.' Gunnar looks stunned, so the Archbishop repeats: 'Make me an example and I will return to look at it. Tomorrow. Come, Jarl Magnus.'

The Archbishop's tall, dark-haired advisor is the last to leave the workshop, just as I rise from my hiding place. He is the one they talk about, the Archbishop's right-hand man. Our eyes lock for a moment. I see kindness there, unexpected. *I wonder what he sees in mine. Fear? Guilt?*

Or can he see the determination of a boy with a plan?

With a swish of the door cloth, he is gone.

The Southern Isles. The place from which my mother and I were taken in a raid. She was pretty and I looked strong enough, they said as they dragged us towards their longship. I was but seven winters old. I was sent to the workshop and she became a maid to a young noblewoman. Soon my mother was sent back, accompanying her young mistress once more to the Southern Isles on the occasion of her marriage. Mother spoke the Gaelic. She may not have had a choice, but she returned, leaving me behind. When she took her hurried leave, her cheeks were wet as she whispered to me. 'The Isle of Lewis. It's your home, Kylan. Never forget it.'

'You'll be back, Mother,' I stated and asked, all in the same breath.

She pushed a strand of the red hair we share from

her forehead and bent down close. 'I hope so. But I don't know. No one knows. It's all in the hands of the Almighty now.'

Thralls. Her and me. She on a ship bound for the most treacherous waters of the known world, me bound to chisel and sweep, polish and carry for the workshop. Both our waters are muddied.

She turned then, pulled her woollen cloak around herself and ran towards the harbour before her mistress sent someone to hurry her along. I stood and stared, watching her fuzzy figure make her way down the hill. I watched until her longship was brushed out by the distance and the night.

I never saw her again.

Now I can barely remember what she looked like.

But I do remember the hand on my shoulder as Old Erik appeared behind me on the shore.

That night, my heart began to carve the beginnings of a plan.

3

THE LONG, LONG NIGHT

No one will sleep tonight. Gunnar and Old Erik are discussing the design. They have opted for chessmen. Any household of standing will have a set of tables-men for Hnefatafl, but chess is new and very fashionable, they say. I thank my lucky stars that I overheard the merchants talking about this new game, down at the trading station where I pick up the raw materials for carving. Wood is easier to work with, but walrus ivory is tough and lasting. One trader had a wooden set of chess pieces out on display, stained crimson and gold and fit for a king. I hear things. See things. It's one of the advantages of my position, and there are few blessings in the life of a thrall.

All this may yet help me with my plan.

But how am I going to stow away on a galley? The ship is not big enough for me to be undiscovered for long. And if they find me, they will kill me; simply throw me overboard, that goes without saying. I need a better plan.

And then it comes to me like a phantom in the dark.

Gaelic. I have some Gaelic.

Master Gunnar's demanding voice slices through th dusty workshop. 'Thrall! Wash this.'

I run over and he hands me a square piece of walru tusk. The outline of a bishop, sitting on a throne, roughly scratched out on the outside. I weigh it in n hand—it is heavy enough. It feels solid. I study tl chiselled outline. Staring eyes, mirrored lines. It look little similar to the wooden chess set I saw at the tradi station, but this is a bishop! Master Gunnar may harsh and hot-tempered—some of his drinking frier say that if he had been born in the saga days, he'd h been a berserker. I smile at the thought. Gunnar's Sa How funny that sounds. But he is a genius. A be carver has not been found in Trondheim or anywh else, if our steady stream of customers is anything t by. Old Erik trained him, but it is Gunnar who pe want. *Einar is tolerable*, they say, *but give me Gun* Gunnar works magic with a chisel and a carving kn

And here is the evidence, right before us on workbench. Of course, he has to include a king a queen—but bishops—in chess? The set I saw h runner, a simple upright shape with a head, but no features. *What is Gunnar doing?* He carves a face, a human face. It even has hair, and a mitre of the kir bishops have just started wearing. I am sent to ref

bucket and wash it clean under the clear water of the hill spring behind the workshop. Suddenly, all the detail shows. The Archbishop is going to be impressed!

Old Erik nods approvingly as Gunnar makes the first few cuts, self-assured and confident, as if one false move could not lose us the best job of the year. His tongue protruding slightly from the corner of his mouth with the concentration, he cuts away beneath the chin and shapes the head wearing the mitre. Next, he adds the folds of the bishop's cope all by previous design. He creates stability for the piece with a seat and a curved crozier, the curled staff all bishops hold as a symbol that they are the shepherds of the church.

Back and forth I run, fetching ale for Gunnar, then a bowl of fish stew, then a whetstone for his carving knife and finally a hunk of bread. Candles for him to see by, too. Later, I drape a blanket over his shoulders as the moon rises high above us, and still he carves, polishes, curses and smiles. His love for the carving art is stronger than his love for his own wife, I am sure. All the others have left now. They recognise that Gunnar is their hope of securing the Archbishop's approval. Halfway through the darkest hours, he discards a figure and starts anew, but he is quicker this time, the knife finding its lines almost by itself. My pile of straw looks so tempting, but I don't lie down either. Instead, I am enchanted by the discarded shavings of ivory, reflecting the candlelight

like sparks as they fly. At sunrise, Gunnar sends me out for fresh spring water. 'There must be no dust in the water at all—the cuts need to be clean. I need to see every imperfection,' he mutters gruffly.

Forgotten is his anger and his temper. Here is a man who is transformed by the knife in his hand. It becomes part of his body, part of his eyes. He sees what he wants to create in his mind and his fingers simply obey and make it happen.

I bend down to pick up the figure he discarded. Ah, I see what he means: he has made a cut too deep across the face, a slash on the left cheek of his bishop. It is a simple slip of the knife, but Gunnar is not interested in anything *nearly* perfect. Flawless is the only thing which will do.

Haltingly, I reach for a knife and look over my shoulder. He is absorbed, despite a sleepless night. The glow of the morning washes into the workshop, and no one else is here yet. Will I risk it?

I place the blade of Old Erik's carving knife diagonally across the flaw and apply pressure.

I expected it to be easier—the way Gunnar makes it look. But no, it takes all my strength to push the knife across to even out the surface. Now the other side, to balance it. He looks thinner than Gunnar's bishop, but decidedly human too. I make a small incision and hollow out the mouth a little to form lips, carefully pulling down the corners of the mouth as I saw Gunnar do. Holding my work away from me to inspect it, I nod without realising. Not bad for a first attempt. I may never get a chance like this again.

When footsteps sound out on the path, I hide the half-finished figure in my pile of straw and cautiously walk back to where Gunnar is applying the final polish to his chess piece. My breath is all but taken away.

As usual, his work is exquisite. But considering this is the work of but one night, the man is nothing short of a miracle worker. Einar and Old Erik clearly agree. 'This is skilled work indeed!', 'Look at the features!' and many more exclamations of admiration ring out, from these men who know great craftwork when they see it.

I stand back a little from the group. I am not one of them, however much I may wish it. The backslapping and horn-bashing until ale slops over the side is not for me. For me is the broom and the pail. But also a plan, secretly stored and hidden in my mind.

And they cannot touch that.

4

THE RETURN

I have to be careful—If I am sent away before the bishop's retinue appears, I will miss my chance. In my mind, I rehearse the sentences and sounds of the Gaelic, as my mother taught me. It anchors me, speaking it under my breath while polishing a newly cut and dried piece of ivory before the men set to work. Running messages to the trading post, I sing a Gaelic song, but I sprint back as fast as I am able. There in the distance by the workshop, looming in the mist, is the company of men I have been waiting for. The Archbishop himself, Jon Birgersson, is among them again; I hadn't dared hope for that, but he is there! Beside him, the advisor who looked straight at me yesterday, and a few other men I do not recognise, armed and ready to defend this most important man in our country's Christendom. *Does he have enemies?*

You can't get to his station in life without enemies.

I need to play my pieces right. Another moment like

this may never come.

Slowly, I edge into the workshop, just after the men. I have to say, the craftsmen's presentation is well-thought out. Someone has draped a scarlet piece of fine fabric over one of the strawbales in the workshop and on it sits the figure. The midday sun streams in through the window and illuminates the ivory bishop as if in a heavenly light. For a moment I forget why I'm here. All the craftsmen stand waiting deferentially. An order like this would keep them all in beer and saltfish for a year, and they know it.

The Archbishop walks towards the display, his cope billowing, leaving straw and dust swilling in the air in his wake. 'Let's see this chessman.'

He bends down. His body is thin and steely under the weight of the clothes and his eyes are bright, catching the light. For a brief moment, I see the carved bishop reflected in his grey eyes. 'Bishops? As part of a game?' he asks.

Gunnar steps forward. 'Yes, Archbishop. Instead of the runners, bishops would look right beside the king and queen on the board, would they not?'

'Ah, yes. I suppose they would.' The Archbishop nods approvingly and walks around the bale to see the back. He gasps, just as I knew he would. An interwoven snake-like pattern decorates the reverse of the ivory piece, with immense care taken over parts of the figure only seen by its player.

It is enough. Archbishop Birgersson turns to his advisor.

'Carve me these gaming sets and have wooden boards made to accompany them.'

As one, the craftsmen give a sigh of relief, but maybe I am the only one to notice it.

'We shall have five gaming sets made,' the Archbishop announces. 'I am taken with the idea of ivory bishops beside the king. It is fitting for the purpose of my journey. Can it be done in time?'

Old Erik and Einar shoot Gunnar a worried look. *Can it be done? So many figures, by the turn of the moon?*

'It shall be done, and with time to spare,' declares Gunnar confidently, without as much as a sideways glance.

'So be it. My advisor Jarl Magnus will see to your needs.' The Archbishop strides out and mounts his cart, pulled by two Icelandic ponies and driven by two men. His advisor lingers inside to weigh out hacked silver pieces for Gunnar to pay for materials. Soon the hoofbeats sound ever more distant on the path back to the cathedral. The advisor is finished and makes to leave. I dart to the doorway to hold the curtain back and Old Erik shoots me an approving glance. I can only imagine what the craftsmen must think when I scramble out after the man and sprint to his horse.

'Jarl Magnus,' I begin, out of breath with nerves. 'I can

speak the Gaelic. I am good at it. Fluent in fact. I'll be useful on your journey, should it please you to take me.'

He stops and I look at him properly. He has an unreadable face, and someone so ruddy and dark-haired is unusual for these shores. His shoulders are broad and, while not nearly as muscular as Gunnar's or Einar's, his arms are certainly strong. He wears the garments of the church like a man might wear a child's cloak, with a little embarrassment. His beard—unusual for a churchman to have one—is pleated at the side. He is silent; it is impossible to guess at what he is thinking.

I retreat, resisting the powerful temptation to look back to the workshop. In the distance, we can see the rest of the Archbishop's entourage disappear down the hill and take the turning to the cathedral instead of the harbour.

He bends down to me. 'You are a Scotus by birth?'

'Yes, sir. My mother and I were taken in a raid. But my mother spoke to me in the Gaelic tongue every day.'

He clears his throat. 'We already have a man to translate. A scholar. Your place is in the workshop… *thrall*.' He emphasises the last word, the final blow. The end of the conversation.

'I don't eat much,' I try in desperation. 'I am useful and strong and quick to understand, and I have courage and…' I run out of words to praise myself. *Who am I trying to fool?* The man is already swinging himself onto his horse with great grace, unlike the Archbishop who needed two men to haul him out of the cart, with all his heavy garments.

The advisor does not answer. Instead, he gestures at the workshop where the door cloth has been drawn aside and Old Erik stands, beard and long greying hair blowing sideways in the wind.

I was the boy with a plan. Now I am the boy with nothing.

Thankfully, when I return to the workshop, Einar and Gunnar are still celebrating. I can feel the old craftsman's eyes boring into the back of my head. Of course, he will want to know what on earth I could have been doing, speaking to the Archbishop's advisor unasked. I am supposed to be invisible, like a bucket in the corner, like a barrel at the trading station. I am a possession, a boy without a choice. *So why do choices and longings torment my mind? Why?*

I sigh and begin restoring the workshop to what it was before the visit, pulling workbenches and stools and tools back where they belong. Gunnar is back-slapped and shoulder-patted out of the door to take a day at home in his bed, and I breathe a little deeper. The workshop is a kinder place when Gunnar is not around.

I will remain. No more to be said.

The day turns out the busiest in my memory. The

Archbishop's advisor paid us a large deposit, but we will immediately have to spend it on more walrus tusks if we are to make the five sets of chess pieces required.

'Here, Kylan,' Old Erik says, handing me a pouch of silver. He is the only one of them to ever call me by my name. 'Go to the traders and tell them to ask around. We will buy every last walrus tusk to be had in Trondheim. If necessary, we will buy from other towns along the coast. We will pay handsomely. Pass that message on.'

He hasn't mentioned anything about this morning, which means he has forgotten, or he is not as suspicious as I thought. I am grateful.

'Oh, and Kylan…'

My hand suddenly feels clammy around the bunched end of the money-bag.

'I saw you talking to the Archbishop's man today.'

'Erm, yes. He asked me to hold his horse.'

'It looked like a longer talk than that.'

Sweat builds up on my forehead. 'Did it? Oh, he asked about my accent.'

I am well aware that my accent is almost imperceptible. I do not sound like a foreigner here and Old Erik knows it.

'The Archbishop's man must have good ears.'

I clear my throat. 'Yes, I was surprised too.'

But Old Erik is not done yet. 'I saw him shaking his head, Kylan. As if he was denying you something.'

Swallowing takes some effort. 'He expressed disbelief that I should speak as eloquently as I could, being nothing but a workshop thrall.' I lower my head to hide my laboured breathing.

Old Erik nods, satisfied, if not wholly. 'Run on. There is a ship coming in, see? If it has walrus tusks, you must be the first to ask for them.'

I sprint down the hill, the bag clinking and scraping in my hand.

5

THE CHESSMEN

We are in luck. Solid silver in the hand of the seller will always speed a deal. The trader suspends his foldable bronze scales from the weighing hook in the trading station and places my hacksilver in one pan, adding enamelled lead weights to the other until it is finely balanced. The corners of his mouth creep up. It is enough.

I borrow the trading station's cart and pull the heavy load up to the workshop, to cheers and bustling activity when I return. Despite my failures, they trust me. More than a thrall should be trusted.

'Let's cut them, slave.'

We take no chances this time: Einar and I lift the heavy tusk onto the bench together and fasten it. These men are hard workers and hard drinkers, but they are also gifted by God, make no mistake. I ponder this for a moment. We are all good Christian men, but we love the tales and sagas, too. Tales of the old gods, of Thor and Loki, of Asgard and Valhalla. I can see that they are stories, but I'm told that in the countryside, these tales are still cherished, and they bury their dead the old Viking way.

Sawing through this tusk takes effort and precision. Cut it in a certain way, and the ivory will splinter and crack, wasting all the raw material. My eyes are drooping now—I also stayed up all night—but this does not occur to anyone else, so best not to think about it.

Near dusk, Gunnar returns for a meeting.

'Four of each for each game, apart from king and queen,' begins Einar, scratching runes into a piece of wood to keep track. 'Eight queens, eight kings, sixteen rooks, sixteen bishops, pawns—'

'Wait,' says Gunnar, his eyes sparkling. 'What if we carve warders rather than rooks? Berserkers, even?'

Einar hesitates. 'It will take longer…'

Gunnar reaches across the table and scratches an image into the wood. All bend over to see.

How does he do it? It is nothing but a drawing: a bearded warrior, eyes wide and staring, with a shield pulled up to his face and his teeth biting on it like an animal. It is perfect. You'd feel a little invincible each time you move your piece across the board, surely. But I recognise that glint in Gunnar's eye too, an enthusiasm that won't be denied. A berserker as a warder! The chess set which impressed me so at the trading station now seems very dull in comparison.

As the men list all that needs to be done, the conversation dies down. They realise what will be required. None of them will see their wives between sundown and sunrise. They will have to sleep in the workshop.

'Thrall, go get some ale while we work out what to do.'

The barrels of ale are kept in a cellar near the entrance of the workshop, so I can still hear them, although they speak freely in front of me anyway, as if I didn't exist. Rolling the barrel in with my right arm, I balance drinking horns on my left. Barrel secured, I take a hammer to the tap, hammer it in and hold the drinking horn beneath to catch the first spout of amber liquid. I have had plenty of practice. As soon as the final horn is filled, I tip the barrel upwards so that none of the precious drink is wasted.

Old Erik gives me an appreciative look on my return and addresses the younger craftsmen. 'So, it is decided. We will make smaller sets of the ends of the tusks, and bigger sets from the widest parts. There are not enough of us though. Even if all three of us were to devote all daylight hours to this work, it could not be done, could it?'

Einar looks at Gunnar, his eyes searching. 'Do you think...'

Gunnar frowns. 'There aren't many who possess enough skill for this kind of work… and I know what you're thinking, Einar.'

I am bewildered. *What do they mean? They are speaking in riddles!*

Gunnar shakes his head, as if to awaken himself from a bad dream. 'Maybe you're right. Let's ask.' Gunnar gives a big sigh. 'I have a feeling we will live to regret this.'

Einar shakes his head. 'Gunnar, we have no choice.'

All the others nod solemnly.

A decision has been made and I have no idea what it is.

I don't get an opportunity to dwell on it. Old Erik sends me to the trading station with yet more silver. 'Find a rider messenger, make him swear by the old gods and the new to deliver it by sundown, and remember his name, whatever you do. Hurry!' He presses another rune-marked wood into my hand.

Gunnar barely acknowledges me when I return. He is chiselling his first king, tongue firmly in the corner of his mouth again. I thought he'd look more pleased, but a grunt is all I get for my troubles. My lids weigh heavily as I slouch outside to fetch more water for washing the dust out of the cuts on the figures. I have barely caught my breath today. Coming back into the workshop, I hear Gunnar sigh deeply.

Old Erik has sidled up behind me. 'Pay him no heed,

Kylan,' he says gruffly. 'It's grief and jealousy and pride, that's all that's ailing him.'

It is not my place to ask questions, so I don't. But I do pray to the Almighty to grant me a plan once more. All night, amid fitful sleep, I glance across at Gunnar as he scratches, carves and polishes before carving some more. There is a smile playing about his lips and I am glad. He sets his king upright in the candlelight and stretches before blowing the candle out and rolling himself up in the pile of straw at the foot of his workbench. Einar has gone home as he has an ailing mother and a wayward son. Old Erik has fashioned himself a small makeshift hut, only a stone's throw from the workshop. All is quiet. A mouse scurries along the workshop floor, but that is all. I rest my eyes a little until strong snores fill the room.

In the dead of night, I rise and creep across to Einar's workbench, reaching for the finest of his chisels. I have watched and I have learned. *Could I be as good as Gunnar, one day?*

Unless I try, I will never find out.

If I'm caught, I'll get a beating. Bruises heal.

Should I not take my chance when opportunity favours me? I may grow to despise myself, and that sort of wound may never heal at all. With new resolve, I retrieve the part-carved ivory hidden in my straw and place the chisel against the figure. I close my eyes for a moment to see the design in my mind once more and begin, holding it up so the moonlight catches it. Over by the workbench, Gunnar rustles in his sleep. His fingers twitch. He must be carving in his mind. And, like an apprentice, I make the movements he would make, the cuts he would cut, the holes he would drill. He does not know it, but he is training me, here in the dark.

I am a craftsman in the making. It is all part of a new plan, a plan for a future in which I have some skill and a way of making a living as a free man. If the plan fails, I will fail with it.

The screech of a barn owl outside distracts me for a second and I realise: like my master, I have placed my tongue in the corner of my mouth.

6

WOMEN IN THE WORKSHOP

I wake with a start and bang my head on the beam above my sleeping corner. The noise makes Gunnar stir, too. I realise, to my horror, that I still have the half-carved bishop figure in my hand. Einar's chisel has slid to the ground in my sudden movement. The metallic ring on the stone floor would be enough evidence of my guilt, but Gunnar seems unaware. He seems much more interested in the door. Someone is standing outside; I can tell by the outline. Quite a small man, I think.

'Thrall, check.' *That's right, Gunnar, never waste ten words on politeness when two will do.* I jump to my feet, hide the tool in the folds of my garment and then soundlessly slide it onto Einar's workbench as I pass. Gunnar's eyes are still fixed on the doorway. I turn and look properly. If I didn't know any better, I'd say there was something uneasy in his guarded face. Even fear.

'Do as you're told,' he bellows, and at that point I know

for certain: Gunnar Gunnarsson is scared of whatever is on the other side of that leather curtain. I gulp and push it aside a chink. Outside, framed by golden morning mist, stands a small woman. Her lined features are pleasing, I suppose. I don't know why, but she oozes strength. She raises her chin and looks down on me.

Is she waiting for me to speak?

It seems she is. Just as I open my mouth, I notice a movement behind her. She has a girl with her. Dressed in ordinary clothes, but certainly not from Trondheim, of that I am fairly certain.

'Aren't you going to ask us in?' the girl says haughtily.

'He is a thrall. Can't you tell, Freya? Don't speak to him. GUNNAR!'

Her voice startles me so much that I withdraw right back into the workshop where Gunnar sighs, biting his lip.

'It is her. I did not think she'd answer the message.' He says it aloud, before realising that the only one to hear is me. He hides it well though, reaching for his work tunic and smoothing his wild hair down, just as the two strangers decide to invite themselves right in. There have never been women in here, not ever. The girl strolls past Einar's bench, lifts up the chisel and inspects it in the light of a sunray. The sunlight glitters in her eyes like the sparkle of a wave. Why does the woman not keep her child in check?

It's because she is distracted, I think. She glares up at Gunnar, the most intimidating man I know, and folds her arms in front of her chest, standing broadly before him. Gunnar stretches himself up to his considerable height, but looks away, just past her face. 'Margrét hin haga. You came.'

'I know my own name. Why did you call for me?'

'You look well. It has been a long time.'

'Don't sweet-talk me, Gunnar. What's your game?'

At this, a smile begins to creep into Gunnar's expression. 'I heard you were in Trondheim with your husband.'

'And my daughter. Yes. What of it?'

'It seems fortuitous. I know that your skill with a carving knife is legend, even here across the waters.'

'In my own Land of Ice and Fire, yes, my work has received some praise.' She holds his stare.

'I know your husband has come from Iceland to pay his respects to the new Archbishop. The same Archbishop who will soon make the journey to the Southern Isles.'

'And what is any of this to do with me?'

Gunnar's tone becomes urgent: 'Work for me, Margrét, just for the next two weeks. I will pay you handsomely.'

'You know I work alone.' The woman turns her face away and motions for her daughter to join her. I'd wager that the girl is about the same age as me, but irritatingly, she is a hand's width taller. I bet she is fed meat and milk though, not just water and fish stew.

'No matter; suit yourself,' answers Gunnar, but he does not sound defeated yet, and that makes the woman pay attention. 'We have a commission to carve chessmen. Gaming pieces of the latest fashion. Like this one for example, or this one. But if you're not interested…'

He turns away, but the woman hasn't moved. It's as if Gunnar had cast a spell by flaunting the two finished figurines. The air is still; the woman's breathing is shallow. After what feels like an eternity, she moves forward. 'Gunnar the Knife, your skill has grown since we learned together.'

'At that time, you were the better carver, Margrét. But then you went back to your home in Iceland. When we heard you were here on your husband's business—'

She reaches for the figures, and to my surprise, Gunnar yields them gladly.

Margrét stares at the chess king in her hand. 'The crown. What tool did you use?' Gunnar holds up the twisting drill piece.

'How did you secure the figure?'

He holds up the vice which slots into the workbench.

'And the design on the side of the throne?'

'My own.'

'Your own?' Gone is the tough bravado and the confrontational tone. Here is a woman who has stopped seeing the workshop, her daughter, the craftsman or me. All her attention is on the figure. Admiration—and something like love—flickers across her features. I have seen that look before, in Gunnar's eyes. Einar and Old Erik are master carvers too, but never have I seen them as spellbound.

'I've begun. Here are some drawings. The others are carving the pawns and some tables-men for Hnefatafl.'

'What needs done?' Her whisper is barely audible.

'We have two weeks. The Archbishop wishes to make a gift of the pieces to noblemen and bishops on his trip to the south. He'd asked for crozier heads and plaques.'

She snorts a little. 'Yes, he would.'

'But we persuaded him to consider gaming pieces.'

'Did you break some tusks?' Her question is like an arrow, quick and piercing and I find myself physically ducking.

'The Scotus thrall boy did. Thankfully, Erik suggested chess pieces.'

Something inside me balks at the injustice—it was my idea—but what is the use of arguing? To the woman I am all but invisible anyway. The girl, however, scrutinises me much more closely than is comfortable.

Gunnar continues: 'We need to design a queen to accompany the king in each set. Warders, bishops, knights—have you seen chess sets before?'

'None like this,' she answers, running her fingers gently over the piece of wood with Gunnar's initial drawings.

She considers it for a moment before speaking. 'I'd pleat the hair. I'd fold the cloak. For stability of the ivory, I'd seat her and lean her arm across like this.'

She is brazen, crossing out Gunnar's initial design and adding her own. She, too, is skilled in drawing and writes the runes quickly, just as words pour from her mouth.

'What are you doing?' The girl has wandered over to my sleeping corner and fingers through my spare tunic and the straw beside it. I shoot over and have to resist the urge to push her away. She squares up to me like her mother did to Gunnar.

'What's it to you? You're a thrall; I know that. I'm free to touch and look at whatever I want. She picks up a handful of my sleeping straw and lets it rain to the workshop floor.

'I'll have to sweep that up,' I stammer through gritted teeth.

'What of it? You've nothing else to do.' She looks at me defiantly. 'You can ball your fists all you like. The adults are taking no notice. Look, if I want I can even—'

'NO!'

But I'm too late. She swings her leg back and kicks my bedstraw right across the workshop. The broken straws look like a thousand Thor's lightning bolts as they sail through the air, showering both of us in grassy fragments. But I'm much more concerned about the half-carved figurine of ivory which skips and chips across the flagstone floor, coming to a wobbly halt just at Gunnar's feet.

7

DISGRACED

That moment, just as the one my mother left, will be frozen into my memory for as long as I live. Rage and comprehension on Gunnar's face, incredulity on the woman Margrét hin haga's—and a moment of regret in the girl's features. But it's too late. I have been found out.

In my mind, I go through the possibilities. I will be beaten, if I'm lucky. I've seen thralls drowned for less than thievery. This may be the end. Slaves are there to do their masters' bidding. A thrall who does anything else is better dead.

There is plenty of cruelty around, despite the cathedral and the prayers. Cruelty is valued as a strength, not shunned, even in these Christian days. All those centuries of Norse domination are hard to undo. The Norsemen love a hero. They love a cut-throat. They love a berserker who loses his temper. I've never dared to set foot in the cathedral, but I have heard that the

Archbishop is a learned man, a gentle soul. How long he can last in this world of warriors is anyone's guess.

All these thoughts race through my mind in mere seconds. But now that Gunnar's steps fall heavily across the floor towards me, I confess my sins and prepare to meet my maker. Just in case.

'Gunnar. Wait. Look at this.'

I flinch, but by the time Gunnar's fist makes contact with my body, it's a weakened, half-hearted blow. Even as such, it sends me staggering against the beam, and I sink to the floor groaning.

'You stole the figure?'

'No! No, I didn't. I never took it out of the workshop. But I hid it, the damaged figure you discarded. I did do that.'

'Gunnar, look!' The woman dares to put her hand on my master's shoulder and yanks him back, such as her strength is, shaking him in the process. 'Beat him or drown him if you wish—but look first.'

She holds my own figure up, the bishop which Gunnar began and discarded after a single slip of the knife. At that time, there were no features, just the rough beginning of a face. Now there is a nose, two staring eyes, a garment of folded cloth and a crozier in his hand, just as I saw it in my mind's eye. My piece's cloak is not a patch on the regular, flowing pattern Gunnar made—but pleasing in its own way all the same. The face is smooth, the mouth pulls downwards, if in a lopsided way. Its other hand is raised in a gesture of blessing. My idea.

'I slashed the face on that figure. I remember it! How can this be?' Gunnar croaks.

I clear my throat. 'I fixed it. I filed it inwards. His face is less plump, I know, but we may yet use it.'

'You had no right!'

'I know.' I hang my head.

'What made you do it?' This time the voice belongs to the woman. It is almost kind, and that, above all else, makes my eyes well up. I despise myself for my weakness but regain control when I feel the hand of the girl on my arm. She got me into trouble in the first place! It probably isn't wise, but I shake her off, more roughly than I probably should.

'Thrall! What made you do it?' The woman repeats.

'I don't rightly know. I wanted to carve. I thought I might be able to. I've got a sharp eye, and I'm good with my hands.'

'Have you been trained?'

'No, he has NOT!' Gunnar answers for me. 'Of course he hasn't. But he has watched us; I have noticed that. Erik doesn't mind him near.'

Margrét hin haga holds the piece to the light. 'It's promising.'

'The slave should not have touched our work. He deserves punishment,' Gunnar spits.

'He does,' she agrees. I sink into myself. 'But he could be useful, too. Five sets, and just yourself, Erik, Einar and me.'

He doesn't have an answer to that, so the woman continues. 'Even if we get through the chess pieces, we need help with the pawns and the tables-men. Think about it, Gunnar. Any thrall needs to know his place, yes, but think! A raw talent like that, beneath your very eyes which you discard at your peril. What would the Archbishop do if the sets were not complete?'

Gunnar looks cross and mumbles. 'What do I know?'

'You know very well! He would sail south to Scotland and purchase another gift from a trader on the way.'

There is silence in the workshop. The only movement is the head of the girl, swivelling from me to her mother to Gunnar and back.

At last Gunnar sighs. 'Oh, very well. Erik will be pleased. He has been asking to train the boy for months.'

If this morning had not been so remarkable in every single way, I would surely have fainted at this suggestion, but now I merely redden with embarrassment and pleasure. Train me? It is what I dreamt of—what I hoped for.

Another piece of my plan slots into place.

8

THE CATHEDRAL

My blisters are healing and crusting over slowly. A week has passed since that oddest and most wonderful of mornings. Margrét and her daughter Freya have been in the workshop almost constantly, although her husband sends soldiers to escort them home every night. Now I'm on my way to the Archbishop's residence beside the cathedral with a message. We are on track to complete the figures, but we will need to buy more ivory. A trading ship has just pulled into the harbour. If the Archbishop will give us another advance, we can make good the order.

Work on the cathedral has been going on for as long as I can remember, but its octagon shape stands tall. Worshipping there is a luxury for the free, not the slaves. But I send a prayer to heaven every time I pass it, in the hope that the Almighty will catch in on the wind. *What for?* It's a prayer for my mother. A prayer—dare

I wish it?—for freedom and a life of my own making. Prayers for Old Erik who is kind, but often sad. Prayers for protection and for strength in illness too. A prayer for hope.

That particular prayer seems to have been granted. Hope has clawed its way into my heart and made its home in it. One day, I shall go to the Southern Isles and find the Isle of Lewis. I shall be free. I shall find my mother and die happy. All else is not important.

It looms above me, the large structure of the cathedral. I clutch my thin sheet of wood with scratched runes on it. Often, the monks and priests sing chants when I pass, giving my ears the ring of heaven, but it is silent today. The heavy wooden door is ajar.

Curiosity gets the better of me. Uncertainly, I stare at the wood in my hand. A few minutes won't make a difference, will they?

I look all around me. Something draws me to the cathedral, the dwelling place of the Almighty. Old Erik doesn't believe that. '*See the fjords shimmer, Kylan? See the Northern Lights in the sky during winter nights? See the rays of the sun sparkle in the dew in summer? The Almighty is in all of it, Kylan.*'

But this is the house which the best craftsmen of the Northlands are building for their God, and I can't help it: I want to see it from the inside.

I tiptoe in, fearful of being spotted, and am taken

aback by how cool and dark the interior is, with arched ceilings, vaulted high as heaven itself. There are carvings and paintings of saints and sinners, of heaven and hell too. I shudder. Step by step, I walk past the benches and prayer cushions on the stone floor, barely breathing. My eyes are drawn upwards, upwards to the glory of the building and to the glory of God. Who could walk into such a building and not be praying?

I am about to sink to my knees for a precious moment when I realise: I am not alone.

I fight the urge to run once I grasp who my fellow pilgrim is.

The Archbishop's right-hand man, Jarl Magnus, is lying face-down on the floor of the cathedral, in front of the altar.

At first, I fear he is dead, so still does he lie. Should I get help? But no, he is speaking, mumbling. He has not seen or heard me—of that I am sure—he would never speak thus in front of a thrall.

It is a croak more than a voice: 'Forgive me, Almighty God. Forgive this sinner before your throne.'

His throat repeats the word *forgive* another five or ten times. It is more mesmerising than a skald telling tales of monsters and magic. These are private words between a man and his maker.

I shouldn't be here.

I will edge out of the doorway the way I came and run

to the palace with my message. *Nearly there.*

But walking backwards comes with its own perils. My tunic sleeve catches on the edge of a candlestick as I move, pulling it with me for a thumb's length, but it is enough to produce a screeching sound on the ground. The praying stops abruptly. In my frantic haste to disentangle the cloth, the candlestick topples over with a clatter. The sound echoes around the cold stone walls for some time. All caution forgotten, I run towards the door. *Away! Away from here.*

'Halt, boy!'

I consider disobeying that order. He is far behind and I could probably outrun most people in Trondheim on the flat. But there is a raw authority in the voice that simply will not be ignored.

I turn, slowly and feel the cold edge of a sword pressed to my throat. It seems the house of God is not a sanctuary for all.

9

JARL MAGNUS

'What did you hear? WHAT did you hear?'

'Good sir, I had a message to bring to the Archbishop's residence. But…'

I falter. Best to be honest. 'I so very much wanted to see the cathedral from the inside, so I took a moment and heard you.' The blade presses harder into my skin. The man's face is flushed above his beard.

I hand him the rune-wood. 'Here. From Master Gunnar. The order is going to be finished, but he is asking for a little more silver in advance, to complete the sets.'

His eyes do not waver and his voice fizzes with fury. 'None of this I asked, boy! I asked: *What did you hear?* Think more carefully about your answer, or my knife will strike true.' He sounds menacing, like a man not entirely in command of all his senses.

'I heard nothing, good sir. Nothing at all of any consequence.'

He knows I heard; he must do. Best to confront it head-on. 'I heard you converse with the Almighty. I turned away as I am nothing but a foreigner and a slave. I shouldn't have intruded.' Slowly, the pressure on my neck eases until the tip of the sword simply hovers a finger's breadth away from my skin. 'I mean you no harm, Jarl Magnus. I can keep quiet.'

If only he knew how often I have had to keep silent in my life. But he seems pacified for now.

I try again. 'Pray take the message. I do not read, but I can take an answer back to my master.'

Thankfully, he steps back and sheathes his sword. He glances over the runes and lifts his face. 'Very well. Tell Gunnar that we will send more silver tomorrow.'

'I will, sir, I will.' With that I make for the door before turning back once more. 'And sir, remember what I said about the translating. In case you need me.'

'We won't.'

But some shadow of thought crawls across his features at that moment. Maybe I have seen him weak and he wants to keep an eye on me. Maybe he is simply thinking of something else.

I should not be speaking to this man of my own accord at all, but somehow, the words keep coming out of my mouth. 'I am helping with the carving, you know. I sometimes fix and repair the pieces when a craftsman has made a mistake. I'd be useful, in case something happens to the precious pieces on the journey.'

'What makes you so desperate to go the Southern Isles?'

'I'm not.' I shrug and look away. The falsehood makes my conscience crawl under my skin.

'Don't lie to me.'

'What made you pray face-down on the ground, good sir?'

I am shocked at my own words and flinch as I say them. I will die now, for sure. The insolence of a thrall asking probing questions of the second most important man in the city! I lower my head.

'It is my business. Mine and the Almighty's.' His low voice boils with rage.

'Then that is my answer to your question too.' At this, I run down the nave, through the door and across the covered walkway. I don't stop till I have left the river far behind and the cathedral and the Archbishop's palace are nothing but roofs poking up behind the lower huts of my fellow men.

'What's got you?'

Margrét's daughter. *What is she doing here?*

'Are you all right? You can hardly breathe.'

'Fine,' I say, annoyed. 'I've got to get back.'

'I'll come with you.'

'No.' How insolent this must sound.

'It wasn't a question,' she answers and gathers her cloak. The wind is not cold anymore, more like a breeze carrying the promise of light.

I sigh and set off at as fast a pace as I can muster, but she keeps up with me easily.

'You have a secret,' she says simply. 'I can tell. People with secrets behave in a certain way.'

'I don't have the luxury, or the time, for secrets,' I snap, but she just laughs.

'I'm Freya. We got off to bad start, didn't we?'

I don't answer.

'And I know your name is Kylan.'

'Please leave me alone.'

'And I just saw you coming out of the cathedral.'

My spine gives a shiver. 'I was delivering a message.'

'You were running from the church. The Archbishop's man came rushing after you and stood on the steps, checking where you had gone.' She hesitates. 'He looked like a man with a secret too.'

I stop and face her square on. 'In that case, maybe we all have secrets. Maybe those with secrets ought to be left alone. '

'I was told to look out for you, you know.'

That gets my attention. 'What?'

'My mother wants me to learn the carving art, but she is not at her best when someone stares over her shoulder. So she told me to watch you instead.'

The last few hundred steps up the hill to the workshop pass in silence. Watch *me?*

Old Erik is waiting. 'The silver will be sent tomorrow,' I say without stopping. I don't want him to scrutinise my face.

The old carver looks relieved. 'Then we can reserve the ivory at the trading station to make sure they do not sell to anyone else. I'll do it now.' He fastens his overcoat and gives his workstation a cursory wipe. He does not need to say anymore; I have already picked up a broom and begin to sweep. He gives me a wink. In the corner, Freya puffs with frustration. Watching me fetch water and clean the workshop is probably not going to make her a carver.

The afternoon, however, is different, for a whole host of reasons.

The sun is high enough for light to stream in even into my small sleeping corner beneath the beam. I am bent over a pawn, the delicate pattern of knots marked out in charcoal. I try hard not to smudge it. The ivory is so precious, it must not be wasted by careless treatment. Behind me, Freya watches and asks endless questions. *Do you have to hold the knife with your right? Do you press hard? What if you cut too deep and the texture changes? Have you done this for long? Are any of the designs your own? How can you stand working with Gunnar when he is so surly?*

I try to distance myself in my mind, hear her questions as if through water and answer only in one or two words to discourage her. I have never heard anyone talk so relentlessly. Gunnar and Einar cast her mother disapproving looks from time to time, but she ignores them, and I am trapped. Until the door of the workshop flies open and he stands in the opening like a bat, his dark cloak floating in the wind.

All of us lower our tools, slowly, assessing the situation.

It is the Archbishop's man. Jarl Magnus. His face is controlled, but he does not look at Gunnar, or Einar or Old Erik. He does not even look at Margrét.

His dark, unfathomable eyes have found me, like a key finds its lock.

10

THE WHEEL OF STARS

'I need to have a word,' he bellows into the silence.

Margrét drops her knife, but no one else moves until Gunnar stretches and walks purposefully to the man, making calming gestures behind his back.

Everyone relaxes a little. Gunnar will sort it out.

Apart from me. I do not relax one little bit.

The two men step outside and I strain my ears. All the rest of them pretend not to care, but there is no chatter and no filing—we all avoid the activities which make a noise. The cursed summer wind has picked up outside, whipping around the corners, obscuring some of the words. But others it carries towards our ears.

'The boy? Have you not heard the tales of redheads, sir? He will be a curse on your journey.'

'I command it.'

'He is mine. With all respect, sir.' Gunnar's voice does not sound particularly respectful; it has to be said.

'Here, consider...' The wretched wind wrestles the rest of the words away, but in a second or so, we can pick it up again.

'It is a dangerous journey, but one which needs to be made. I have my reasons for wanting to take the boy, you will have yours for wishing to keep him. The thing that is going to make the difference is silver. Am I right?'

Gunnar hesitates. 'How much silver?'

We can hear the men beginning to walk away, taking the rest of their conversation with them. Only then do I see that everyone else in the workshop has frozen. Every single one of them is looking at me. I thought I'd be delighted if the Almighty heard my prayer, but instead, by hands are clammy as they reach for the carving knife again. This pawn in my hand has become the only thing I see. *Carve the pattern, wipe it clear of dust. Another incision, wipe it clear.* I discipline myself not to think. Because if I think, I will have to admit that this workshop is the only home I can remember.

Just as if he had read my thoughts, Old Erik puts an arm around my shoulder from behind. He has never done that before; a small moment of kindness among the cruelty.

I turn to give him a watery smile.

An hour later when Gunnar returns, he smells of the celebratory ale of a successful transaction. He carries two purses of clinking hacksilver and drops one on Einar's workbench. 'Here, this is for more ivory. Take the boy to pick it up—it's set aside for us at the trading post.'

Einar nods and wipes his hands and dusty face with a cloth. Einar is an outstanding wood carver, but he has set all of that work aside for the moment to help us with the chessmen. He gives me a nod to get ready, but clearly doesn't want to leave yet—not until Gunnar has explained the presence of the other purse.

'We heard some of what was said, Gunnar,' Old Erik says drily, his eyes drilling into the master crafter's head.

Gunnar shrugs. 'Looks like we need to find ourselves a new thrall for the workshop. This one…' He indicates me with a flick of his head. 'Somehow, this one has found favour in the eyes of Jarl Magnus. Wants to take the boy with them on their journey to the Southern Isles, and who am I to stand in his way? He is a man of influence and of riches.' Gunnar shakes the bag. 'We can take the dark months off after this.' Einar nods at that—the thought is attractive. Gunnar adds: 'He says the boy is sharp and will be useful, though I can't think how. I'll tell you though, I would not like to get on the wrong side of that man. The Archbishop himself is mild, but this dark-haired one—I think he would kill ten men without a thought. You know what I mean? Maybe I'll base my final warder figure on him.'

At this, Gunnar laughs, and Einar laughs with him. Margrét and Old Erik do not. In all of this talk, Gunnar has not looked at me once, or addressed me directly. He speaks about me as if I'm simply another tool in his workshop. He likes it, he wields it, but if someone else is prepared to pay, why not get rid of it? He can always buy another. My throat constricts with jealousy at these free men who can do as they please.

Gunnar leans over his chunk of walrus ivory again and begins to chisel away the excess. I, on the other hand, begin to feel settled. I had a plan. To get away from all of this and to reach the Southern Isles. To be a free man when my time for manhood comes.

Late that night, when I have completed all my tasks around the workshop, I stare up through the small window. The ghostly shape of the barn owl glides across the sky. The moon whirls in a wheel of stars, guiding ships out there at sea. I think of my mother and of the injustice of our capture. Across the field in the feasting hall, free men and boys sit and drink and brawl and plan their summer raiding trips in the ways of old. All of us are fixed into our own wheel of stars, trying to keep our own little corner of the universe lit.

Someone will take my position and, somehow, I have to make a success of my new one.

Pulling the heavy curtain fabric across, I plunge the workshop into darkness.

11

SKALD MAGIC

Just a week later, the workshop is giddy with relief. All five sets of chessmen are finished, including the pawns and a set of tables-men for good measure, as well as folded wooden chequerboards. We finished on Thor's Day past, so Einar, our expert woodcarver, has been busy crafting a suitable wooden casket to preserve the figures in, each in their own velvet pouch lined with clean lambs' wool to keep the chessmen from damaging each other. All of us, in one long procession, make our way to the Archbishop's palace.

I was going to stay behind, but Margrét takes a hold of my tunic and simply drags me along. 'You were part of the making, Kylan. You must be part of the presenting.'

Einar, Old Erik and Margrét stand in line as Gunnar brings the carved casket forward, opening its lid and revealing two or three chess pieces within. The Archbishop himself waits on the stairs of his grand palace to receive them. He looks so splendid in his soft cloak with its silk trim, and with his golden mitre on his head. It is hard to think that this wiry man with such an ordinary name, Jon Birgersson, should hold the reins of Christianity in all these northern parts and all the way to the Southern Isles. I hear that the trip is meant to win over local princes, kings and bishops to his authority. What a far-reaching kingdom the Northlands are! A kingdom worthy of its sagas.

My heart is full. I can barely take in the brief conversation, the nod which the Archbishop gives our small group of craftsmen, the final sack of payment presented by Jarl Magnus. His swarthy complexion and black stubble mark him out in the cold summer mist.

I stay at the back of the group and out of sight—Gunnar would surely lose his temper if he saw that I have come, although Old Erik and Margrét give me a sad smile. Tonight is the feast. And tomorrow?

Tomorrow I will join the Archbishop, Jarl Magnus and their seamen, to sail southwest towards Scotland.

The craftsmen, alongside the rest of the town, will attend the special mass this afternoon to pray for safety of the journey and for the Almighty's blessing on the Archbishop's tenure in the faraway isles, while I and the other thralls prepare the feasting hall.

I pray from a distance as I see Trondheim's karls and jarls shuffle through the wide wooden cathedral doors.

The craftsmen will be included. After all, they made most of the wooden decorations in this great kirk.

I roll barrels of ale and mead in and help the village women to stoke the fires beneath the hog roasts on the spits. Turning meat on three spits takes some watchfulness, and the spit boy, a Teutonic thrall, can do with all the help he can get.

My favourite part of the night is when the skald appears. I love all kinds of sagas and this bald man with his bearskin for a coat is rumoured to be simply the best at telling them. He sets himself up in the corner and I fetch him a drinking horn and a cut of cooked meat.

Eventually, the men file in from mass, slapping each other on the back and daring each other to empty a drinking horn ahead of everyone else. The summer nights are stretching and the sun is teasing the horizon like a cat toys with a mouse: *I'm coming for you. No, I'm not. A little while longer.* Eventually, it does touch down, bathing the entrance to the hall with amber magic and outlining the men with light, as if touched by heaven itself. The feast is noisy and wild, fitting for a farewell. We are not the only ones setting off—there are several trading ships and a handful of warriors from our parts who are joining the Crusades to the Holy Land. The weather looks to stay fair if the wise men of the town are to be believed.

I cast about, but no, neither the Archbishop nor Jarl

Magnus are here. In any case, I am too busy to concern myself with them, running to refill ale and replenishing platters of food on the long table. The craftsmen are all here, and I notice Gunnar has a new set of leather boots after the manner of the rich—I am sure he is putting the money he got for me to good use.

And then it begins. Some of the men take a while to settle but the skald is no blind kitten—he knows exactly how to gather the crowd. First there is a hush.

'The skald is going to tell a tale.'

'Shhh, listen.'

A single chord rings out from the small horsehair harp he carries and we see him at the end of the table, but for a moment. Then, with a swish of his cloak, he is gone. The women gasp, and if I'm honest, I do too, because he suddenly swings himself up halfway along the table and stands on it, high above the rest of us, swinging two burning torches around his head. There is a subtle drumming noise which builds, and I see then that he is making it himself, with his feet, drumming wide-legged on the sturdy table. A platter or two slide to the floor but no one pays them any heed. He suddenly freezes, catches the torches in one hand and passes them to a maiden waiting beside. Pulling the harp from his cloak again, he strums twice or thrice more.

'I know for certain Odin
Where you conceal your eye

In the famous Spring of Mimir
Mead he drinks
Every morning
From the Pledge of the Father of the Slain
Do you know any more or not?'

He sings not. But it is a melodious incantation which casts its spell powerfully over everyone here as he recites the familiar *Völuspá* poem about the old religion and the creation of the world, all sixty verses of it. My lips imitate the sounds, I cannot help it. The skald remembers every rhyme and lives every emotion—and we live it with him. At the end, I stand open mouthed.

A drunk old man stumbles through the crowd and noisily demands more ale before Old Erik—yes, my mild-mannered Erik—simply raises a fist and knocks him to the ground, admonishing him: 'Hark! Hush. The skald is speaking!'

Undeterred, the skald begins again. I am not familiar with the beast in his next tale:

'Long ago, the Stoorworm curled its long and scaly body around the whole earth. It was the oldest, cruellest creature the world ever did see, a true devil in scaly armour, with a body longer than any ship could hope to sail in a Viking's lifetime.'

A small gasp escapes my lips and I see the corner of the storyteller's mouth twitch upwards. But he does not break his flow.

'There was once a farmer's boy. His name was "Ash-raker", Assipattle. Now, when the Stoorworm arrived in the land and demanded his feed of seven maidens each week...'

I hang on the skald's every word, on the sacrifices, on the King's desperate gamble to trust lowly Assipattle to fight the beast, and Assipattle's heroic deeds. I flinch at the final fight where Assipattle sails into the very mouth of the beast with nothing but a pail of burning peat and a newly sharpened knife. The skald lowers his voice with a faraway gaze, as if he were seeing the smoky darkness with his own eyes. I suppose we all are.

'Then Assipattle ran aground inside the darkness of the Stoorworm's stomach, with oily water splashing around his feet. He could barely take a breath in the stench of wickedness, but by the low light of the smouldering peat, he found his way to the beating heart of the creature. A cut. Then another and another. Assipattle placed the burning embers of peat into the hole he had cut and blew and blew and blew—until he had fanned into life a flame so large and so angry that it sparked and sprayed burning oil and Stoorworm blood. The whole of the cavity was shaken by the sudden roar of the creature, enough to split the heavens from the skies for a moment. The Stoorworm gagged and spat, but it could not rid itself of the flames inside. It vomited out as much water as it could, sending Assipattle

and his boat on a foaming wave back to the shore, even as great plumes of smoke rose into the darkening sky.'

The skald halts, assessing his audience. In his presence, all of us are nothing but babes, entranced by his tale. Mighty warriors, muscled labourers, thralls, karls and jarls—all of us willingly surrender to the sway of a saga.

'Assipattle took the hand of the King's daughter in marriage...'

'What of the Stoorworm?' someone shouts from the back.

The skald turns so that the light of the torches dances on his face. *'The Stoorworm? It raised its neck high above the sea in its dying moments, crashing to the ground and smiting its bones. Its teeth were knocked high into the air and rained down into the waves. There they still lie. We call them the Northern Isles, Shetland and Orkney. The beast then curled itself up in a final dying moment. Its body is what we call Iceland, home of the settlers.'*

There is a moment of lingering in the tale. No one speaks; few drink or eat. There is such magic in a story well told, such strength.

Then the music begins and the feast resumes.

I shall treasure this brief moment belonging, with this place and these people. For a season, they have been part of my own saga, and I of theirs.

And if heroic deeds are yet to come, such deeds will unfold as the Almighty sees fit.

12

THE ETERNAL FAREWELL

The following morning, dawn is misty, promising a clear day. There is no sign of the craftsmen as I sweep back my straw pile one last time in the half-light and wrap my tunic closer around myself. Summer may be here, but the sea is cold, and the storm-stirred air above it even colder. I have no warm clothes. I hadn't thought of that.

There is nothing I can do about it anyway. Jarl Magnus may be kind, or he may not be kind. All I know is that he is my master now and my escape plan, such as it is, is coming together. I'm certain that Gunnar and Einar will be drunk for some time still. I saw them both snoring beneath the long table of the drinking hall as I left, with the moon high in the sky.

Hark! A noise.

'Kylan. You can't go without saying goodbye.' It's no more than a whisper and Freya pushes her head through the doorway.

I don't know what to say to that, but I am glad of the company as I straighten up and look around. Not until that moment had I realised how little I own. The clothes covering my skin. Both my hands are free to run through my hair, for I have nothing to carry.

I can tell Freya senses it. Longing and fear. Longing for adventure, and for a future. Fear of the same things.

'When are you sailing?'

'After sunrise,' I say looking around at the unfinished jobs. Someone else's work now.

'Don't worry. Shall we go?'

Without provisions of any kind, I stride down the hill towards the harbour where a large longship is being readied for our journey. Its sleek wooden curves end in a gilded dragon figurehead at the front, but the round-shields lining the gunwale bear the emblem of the cross. The striped sail hangs loosely on the mast, but the flag of the new Archdiocese of Nidaros with its red and gold coat of arms already flutters above it. I suspect that, as with all galleys of this type, we will row and sleep on deck, out in the open. There will be a private chamber for the Archbishop below deck, and perhaps for his scholar too. I can't help feeling a tremble of excitement now.

A huddle of monks shivers by the water's edge, waiting to pray for the Archbishop on his departure, but he is nowhere to be seen yet.

I make myself useful among the seamen, uncoiling

ropes and climbing the mast to secure the sail. We'll have to row out of the harbour and then hoist it to catch the wind. On the harbourside, womenfolk and children are gathering to wave off their menfolk and I turn away.

By now there is a constant line of sailors, entering the ship and carrying provisions, trying out the oar benches and adjusting the handholds. The cleverer ones have brought cloths to wrap around their hands to stop the skin tearing when they take the oars. I've heard so much about seafaring, but I've never had a chance to observe it properly. The smallest thing inspires wonder. Soon there will be larger wonders. I shall see the Northern Isles, Shetland, and Orkney. After that…

The Southern Isles.

'Kylan.' It is Freya's voice again. I thought she had returned to the workshop, but now she waves, on the other side of the gangplank. Beside her stands Old Erik, staring gruffly into the distance, right past my head. 'We've got something for you,' Freya mouths. I push my way down the plank, past the stream of oarsmen. The old carver doesn't look at me, but I swear there is a little sorrow in his eyes and it clenches at my soul to think that the old man cares for me.

'Take this', he croaks. It's a rolled-up garment of wool and dense leather. I am speechless. It is an overcoat after the manner of the warriors. It is a little big on me, but it must have cost him a small fortune.

'Erik,' I begin. My nose tickles and a pressure rises in my throat. 'Oh, Master Erik…' But the sentence simply will not be finished. I don't get a chance to in any case; he interrupts me: 'And this too. In case you have cause to use your skill.'

I feel along the seam of the coat. My heart, full of gratefulness, has no more room, it is fit to burst. 'Erik, your carving knives—and a chisel! Did you conceal them in the overcoat?'

I am overcome.

Old Erik clears his throat. 'I got some new tools for the workshop. A gift from the Archbishop. Let's not forget, you have shown some promise as a carver, have you not? The chessmen may need repairing on the way.'

I am not questioning the new order of the world. At this moment, I feel as free as any man.

'Watch!' Freya pushes me out of the way of an oncoming horse; I am so distracted by the treasures in my hand.

The Archbishop's party, escorted by another ten men, the scholar and Jarl Magnus. The monks begin their prayers while three chests, wooden and copper, are carried onto the boat behind the travellers. Freya says aloud what we are all thinking. 'One of them must contain our chessmen.' The Jarl has dismounted his horse and walks towards us.

'I'd better go,' I say hurriedly, and to be honest, I am

glad. Hurried goodbyes sting less. I hope to see them again in the heavenly kingdom of the Almighty, but I am not likely to return to these shores. This is an eternal farewell.

I swallow. Running across the gangplank after Jarl Magnus, I barely look back and wriggle into my new overcoat, luxuriating in the warmth. What a treasure, what a gift! Clad thus, I do look back, though, and I see Old Erik wipe his face with his sleeve. There are shouts. Ropes are thrown, horns are blown, the Archbishop waves at the crowd with his habit blowing in the wind.

And with a twist of the oars and a gust of the gale, we're gone.

13

THE DANGERS OF THE DEEP

I am glad, so glad, of Old Erik's gift. Without the overcoat, I'm sure I wouldn't have lasted more than a day, even in the so-called fair season. At night, it serves as my blanket while we sleep under the giant wheel of stars, with the sail singing us to sleep. As the waves splash and the breakers roll, I am thrown left and right. Two of the men are sick whenever the motion gets too strong, but I feel no such predicament and simply take their place at the oars when this happens. Jarl Magnus has his eye on me, always. Pain is written in his features. Guilt too. I wonder that such a troubled man is trusted with a position so close to the Archbishop. Once the wind is strong, the oarsmen can rest, letting the sail do our sweaty work. At one point, our galley is all but flying, so burly is the breeze. 'Won't the sail tear?' I ask the Jarl, forgetting that I must not speak, but my head is so full of questions.

'Not this one,' he explains. 'It is the best fabric you can buy, made from wool, and with leather straps to keep its shape when it gets wet. It comes at a comely price too; I can tell you!' He walks away then and I marvel at how he has just treated me, like an equal. I must not get too used to it.

Not long after that, the lookout calls out and points. 'Shetland,' says Jarl Magnus, suddenly beside me again. 'The Stoorworm's teeth. Have you heard the story?'

'I have,' I reply shyly. I'm not sure I want this man to know my deep love of the sagas. I wait for him to say more, to take me back to the tales of heroes and villains, but I am to be disappointed.

'It's only an old tale,' Jarl Magnus says and turns away, mumbling. 'There are other dangers which should trouble us. Real dangers.'

'And what would they be?' I ask almost light-heartedly. Until I see the expression on his face.

I clear my throat and repeat. 'Jarl Magnus! What dangers?'

His brooding look focuses on the horizon in the distance and Old Erik's overcoat suddenly weighs much more heavily on my shoulders. And it's not just the weight of the carving tools, carefully sewn into the hem with linen thread.

A second night on the boat, and I am slowly getting used to the sea. The Archbishop stays in his small chamber below deck while the rest of us brave the elements out in the open. Rain has been light, mercifully, and the waves, I'm told, are tame by comparison to another season. They do not seem tame to me.

I wake in the early morning, with only the tillerman and the watchman alert. Stretching, I raise my head slightly and then wish I hadn't.

Every single patch of me is sore.

But that is not at the forefront of my mind. I can hear something, as if it was emanating from the deep. Without stepping on any of my fellow travellers, I wave to try and attract the attention of the watchman, but only succeed in waking Jarl Magnus who was resting by the mast. In a single, cat-like movement, he is crouching, his eyes darting around. Mysteriously, his hand points at the water, as if he could fathom the foggy deep. The men's snores continue around us, but my senses are on highest alert, as if all my perceptions were balanced on the edge of a sharp knife. My fists clench. Unexpectedly, out of nowhere, a giant spray of brine rises vertically out of the sea, a mere two horses' length from our boat. I cry out.

'It's a giant of the deep,' the Jarl roars. 'Steer away if you can. If you can't, then let the ship float.'

Time stands still. Beside our ship, the sea surface seems to turn brown as it rises, rises, rises. Another jet of water and our boat is pushed backwards and sucked forwards again as a huge—unbelievably huge—fishtail emerges out of the water. It bends upright to the height of our sail and finally curves following its creature down, down, down into the lowest part of the world where no man shall ever tread.

'She'll be down there for some time,' Jarl Magnus says to the men who are all on their feet now, roused by our shouting. 'Set sail and be off. We should reach Shetland today.'

'I am glad of it,' I say out loud, but the Jarl pays me no heed. For the next few hours, I follow the rising sun, reflected on the water, and wonder how such creatures should live and have their being. No one would believe me if I told them about the size of the whale, and the tail hovering above us which could so easily have made kindling of our ship and fish food of us.

But it didn't. It was gentle and slow and majestic, glittering in the watery splendour of the sea. Countless times, I give thanks for God's gift of the journey—for seeing, feeling, hearing and tasting things I have never done before. When raiders took us to Trondheim, we were bound and blindfolded, and I was young in any case. But now, praise be indeed!

When the wind picks up and carries us in the exact direction we want to go, we step away from the oars and relax. I climb the first level of the mast where I like it the best. No one judges me there or asks me questions.

Until I see it in the distance. Unmistakeable: another vessel, making straight for us.

My stomach tumbles and my lungs do something they have never done before: refuse to inhale and exhale. Instead, a strange kind of panting is all I am capable of, with the weight of all the oceans in the world on my heart.

'Raiders!' I shout, but all that emerges from my throat is a croak. The men below are singing and sharing a quick horn of ale before their muscle power is required again, and a couple are relieving themselves over the side of the boat. 'Raiders!' I yell, a little louder, but still no one pays me any heed.

At that moment, the full force of the reality hits me. We are in the middle of the ocean, flying the flag of the rich Archdiocese of Nidaros. Their ship is heading straight for us, making no secret of the fact they mean to engage, and all the while beneath me, men are getting themselves drunk. The other vessel has already grown in size. Soon it will be visible with the naked eye from down on the deck. The Archbishop could be taken for ransom!

It does not bear thinking about. 'RAIDERS!' I scream. This time, my voice cuts right through their jollity and song. These are Norsemen, and fear must have no home in their hearts. But they follow my pointing finger and freeze where they are, if just for a moment. The threat hangs in the sea mist for a second before Jarl Magnus explodes into action. 'What are you waiting for?' he roars. ‘Steer her away. Arm yourselves. Sober up. Your life is forfeit if we surrender the life of the Archbishop whom we took an oath to protect. I will ask him to pray for us all in his chamber below deck. Just as he is raising his hands in prayer, so we must raise our hands in combat. Make ready.’

I cling onto the mast. Our ship’s rudder has been swung all the way to the side, causing the vessel to list dangerously in the sea. At least the waves are calm for now, but there is enough breeze to propel the raiders towards us. Maybe there is also enough wind to propel us away from them?

‘Set sail!’ The command echoes up from below and as I am already in the right position, I try to undo the knot to release the cloth. *Come on.* The rope is glued tight with sea salt and tang, but eventually it gives, even if my fingers bleed. Soon the sail billows in the wind, but a quick glance backwards confirms that the vessel is gaining on us, fast. The fierce painted skulls on their round-shields seem to snarl at our own with their gilded crosses.

14

THE DAGGER IN MY HAND

Where is Jarl Magnus? Hidden, has he? I'm surprised. I thought he looked strong and I didn't take him for a coward, but people surprise us again and again, don't they? I have a better view for judging distance, and there is no doubt about it now: we will not escape this ship. Below me, two of the men lower the Archbishop's flag above the sail, the sign of wealth, but it is too late. Do the raiders mean to strip the ship of its riches and let us go? I find that hard to believe. The Archbishop will be worth more alive than dead. But what of the rest of us?

As the ship approaches, I can see the straggly beards of men who have lived long apart from any kind of company. Their swords are rusty but sharp. There are spears, axes and halberds, and all manner of weapons. At the front, almost leaning over the hull of their galley, are three raiders with coils of rope around their bodies, ready to throw weighted hooks across—and only now do I see what the front of their ship is made of! It's not water glistening on the wood—it's reinforced with iron spikes and they mean to ram us!

'Turn the ship!' I yell down with all my might. 'TURN the ship! We cannot get away. If they ram us, we're done for!'

The tillerman at the stern looks up. He may not have heard everything I said, but I have his attention now. Sliding down the mast as fast as I dare without being thrown into the churning sea, I scream: 'SPIKES! They mean to sink our ship! We have to turn the ship, so we hit theirs broadside.' I use my hands and feet to communicate. The tillerman is not from these parts, but I see his eyes widen with understanding. He pushes the steering oar with the tiller sideways again with all his might. A nearby oarsman rushes to his aid.

Suddenly, I am pulled off my feet backwards, the huge hand of the Jarl on my shoulder. 'Here, boy!'

He thrusts something into my hand, slicing into my palm a little as he does: a dagger, and oh Lord, it is sharp! He doesn't notice or care about the blood, for he is already heading in the direction of the Archbishop's cabin.

I stare at the weapon in my hand. Would I be capable of thrusting this into an enemy's chest? Even if my very life was under threat, I doubt it. But I have no time for dithering: with a terrible clang, a huge metal hook lands over the side of our ship, a rope attached. It tautens almost immediately; the raiders are pulling our ship towards theirs, weapons in hand.

Our men scatter and take refuge, but something possesses me to do exactly the opposite. Darting to avoid the missiles and arrows, I run towards the hooks. This, I am sure, is why the good Lord provided the dagger. I slash at the hook-rope attaching the ships to one another.

They are so close now that I can see the whites of their eyes and when they point and aim all their arrows at me, I duck behind the side of the ship, sawing blindly with only my hand visible to them. I breathe a little easier once it separates and the frayed end with the hook clatters to the deck. But there is another one! Crawling along the oar ports on my stomach, I peer over the gunwale to locate the rope, but they expected me, and arrows hiss over my head. *I must cut the rope, I must.* Hacking, sawing and cutting, I flinch when an arrowhead grazes my hand. I pull back, but I don't drop the dagger. This may not keep them away for long, but I will have done my duty before the Lord and men.

The shouting on both sides is deafening, so deafening that I can't hear a single word anymore, and I wonder that the Archbishop's prayers can be received by the Almighty in this clatter, but I fervently hope they are. With a final gasping effort, this rope, too, snaps. The enemy ship is only two horse lengths away, soon a warrior of strength and stature will be able to jump. Oh no: they are readying themselves!

But then something happens that I have not foreseen. Behind me, there is a commotion; a box is knocked over, heavy footfalls thud on the deck. And then, right past me, Jarl Magnus raises his shield as he runs, mounts the gunwale and, literally, leaps into the air over the whirling waves.

15

THE LEAP

Can he cross the chasm? No, surely.

I've just declared it impossible, but he has done it, landing heavily on the deck across the water. I avert my eyes as the silver curse of his sword flies in a dragonfly circle above his head, while his axe hacks a way through the raiders. *I wonder how many there are.* However, the sound of that moment is the roar! Wounded and raw, his voice carries over the churning sea, the creaking planks, the cries of the wounded and the thunder in the skies.

With an effort, he severs the last of the ropes on the far side and the two vessels drift apart again as the wind fills our sail. Our enemies' surprise is clear. Jarl Magnus hollers, weaving through them all, clanging against shields and slicing into swords. I hang over the side of our own ship, mesmerised by the sheer power of a quiet man, of the sheer courage of the warrior choosing the trap of the enemy ship over his own safety.

But what am I thinking? How is he going to reach us again? He has no hope of returning to us alive, does he? All the oarsmen on our ship are hurrying back to their seats to make good our escape, but I am molten to the side of the ship. Already, it would be impossible to leap back across, even for him. He is a ship's length away, and his arms are tiring, if I'm not much mistaken. There! He has taken a blow to the side and three more raiders are creeping up from the back of the ship, meaning to axe him from behind. 'Jarl Magnus!' I yell, but it's no good. He has saved our lives, but he is going to lose his own.

Then, like a vision clearing in the mist, I see the solution. A rogue wave shakes the ship, but my hands are steady as they reach for our largest curl of rope. In a matter of heartbeats, I sling one end around the mast and through an oar hole, securing myself as I lean against the ship's wall. There are startled shouts.

'JARL MAGNUS!' I cry with all my might and use every muscle, every sinew, every bone and fibre of my body to throw. The sound that comes out of my mouth is like the call of an elk and wolf combined.

I claim this fortune. I long for the success of this simple rescue. My mouth can't form the words, but in my soul, a thousand instant prayers soar to heaven.

Torn by wind and water, the rope flies and uncurls over the boiling sea.

A strong spray obscures my view and then I see—the

rope has fallen just short of the enemy ship! I have failed and sent the Jarl to his death. But then I am shaken by a sudden thud and a splash. Jarl Magnus, sword and all, has jumped into the very waves. A simple breath later, and the rope tautens. Praise be to God! He has got hold of the end of the rope!

'Help me!' I shout to the oarsmen behind me, but they have no ears for me at all—all they hear is the shipmaster and the instruction to row, away and away as fast as they can. 'HELP ME!' I yell again, wedging my thin body against the railing. 'The Jarl hangs by the end of this rope in the waters. I can't pull him up myself! And he is wounded!'

Kicking desperately at the bench in front of me, I finally manage to get someone's attention. The man joins me and we pull, pull and pull again. A wave washes over the side of the ship and sweeps me off my feet, but I claw on, pulling with all my strength. Hauling the warrior clear from the water is the hardest—he is barely conscious and can't help much, but by that time, there are three of us, or maybe four? The raiders' ship is barely a speck in the foaming sea now. They will be busy tending to their wounded.

Three more pulls of the rope. Winding the slack and stopping the slippery hemp from sliding though our raw palms, we heave together. Now we can reach the drenched Jarl; we can't be sentimental, or worry about hurting him further. *Don't think of him as a human*, I tell myself, *just get him into the ship*.

We're utterly spent. *God, give me strength for this!* I grit my teeth, and with a final, grunting effort, the limp and lifeless body of the Jarl Magnus slams onto the deck.

In an instant, I'm on my knees. I pray and press my ear to his face. Closing my eyes, I concentrate hard, and yes, YES, there seems to be a breath. Closing my fingers around his thick-set wrist, there is a heartbeat. Faint, yes, but definitely there. The seascape sways all around me. Bile rises in my throat and I just make it to the gunwale before vomiting into the white-angry surf. Staggering back towards the motionless Jarl is the last thing I remember before it goes dark for a very long time.

16

THE NOBLE GAME

'Where… where am I?'

There are footsteps nearby. Eyes still closed, I try to rise, but my body will not obey me at all! I try something less challenging and thankfully, my finger curls and uncurls on command. Relief. *I am not dead. But what soft thing is this? I have slept on straw all my life, but this—this must be—a bed?*

'Where am I?' I try to pronounce the words more clearly. My mind is a mix of Gaelic and Norse, water and air, dark and light.

'Orkney'. It's a man's voice, gentle and unfamiliar. Or is it? I try to persuade my mind to retrieve it: *where have I heard this voice before?* I push up my eyelids, even if only a chink. A fire glows in the corner. It needs attention, or else it may go out! It's the servant in me, I can't help myself. Even as I try to say so, a figure hushes in—a girl. But not a servant girl, no. Her dress has long sleeves in the manner of the gentry and her red hair echoes mine. She is seventeen or eighteen years of age, perhaps.

'You're in the residence of the Earl Ragnvald Kali Kolsson of Orkney, at Orphir. My father's Bu.'

She shouldn't speak to me at all in that case. What's she doing talking with a slave? I shake my head slightly, but confusion is stubborn and won't be banished. At first, I look for my mother, then for the workshop craftsmen, then for anything familiar at all. *Orkney, yes, part of the Norse kingdom.* Drip by salty drip, the memories trickle back into my messy mind. *The trip. The Archbishop, yes, and Jarl Magnus.* I look across the room and realise there is a padded chair! Padded chairs and beds! There has been a mistake. I resolve to sit up, but invisible ties hold me down and I groan. Jarl Magnus speaks, but my brain has decided not to pay attention to it, however hard I try. Nothing matters but sleep. The girl in the green dress, the bed and the sconces with beeswax candles, the soft blankets and the silence of the air, they all fade into shivery darkness once more.

When I next open my eyes, I am shaken with a fever so fierce—I have never experienced anything like it before.

'We may have to stay a while,' grumbles Jarl Magnus, sitting across from me. 'We missed Shetland.'

'I don't feel well,' I croak and give another shiver.

Any man of sense would have recoiled at that, would

have withdrawn to keep himself safe from any infection travelling on the air, or spread by demons. Jarl Magnus has a strong disregard for what any other man would do. He comes closer.

'Here, drink this,' he offers, thrusting a small waterskin into my hand. I open the vessel and sniff, wrinkling my nose.

'Trust me. You'll thank me. I think about ten of our men are affected by this fever. I'm better now, praise be to God.'

We hear coughing next door.

'The Archbishop Birgersson.' Jarl Magnus continues. 'At least word travelled fast. Apothecaries and medici attended to him quickly and we were all taken away to the Bu of the Earl of Orkney here. It is too dangerous to host fevered visitors at the palace in Kirkwall.'

The girl shakes her hair back. 'My father is there now, overseeing some building work on the cathedral, but he will return soon.'

With this she disappears through the doorway and I am left stunned.

'I have things to do now,' Jarl Magnus growls. 'Drink up.'

I am grateful to be looked after in this way, but also confused and worried. At last my tongue can find the words to express it. 'Are you leaving… me behind?'

'No,' the Jarl says, but his eyes don't smile. 'We need

to wait for the Archbishop to recover. Besides, we may need your language skills yet. The scholar died of the fever yesterday, God rest his soul. Shetland and Orkney are Norse, but in the Hebrides, the Southern Isles, the power is also in the hands of the Gaelic speaking kings. You have a job to do.'

The next morning, I am much better. My eyes are less dull, my muscles still ache, but I still find myself in the bedchamber. I feel like a caged seabird: I need to get out or I'll make a mess. Throwing the blanket back, I take a deep breath and try to rise, even though my head spins a little.

'Not so fast,' comes a voice from the corner. 'You are supposed to rest. Your Jarl commanded it.'

It's the flame-haired girl from yesterday.

'But I need… I need to…'

'Relieve yourself out there.' She points to a corner with a slit in the wall. I obey and do feel a little better. There is a pitcher with water beside, so I can even wash my hands and face.

'Are you any better?'

I nod, amazed at the ease of her manner. She is friendly, certainly, and poised. Her red hair tumbles down one side of her face, held back on the other side by a silver clasp made with extraordinary skill. Maybe I still am a craftsman in my heart.

'I offered to keep watch over you. Your Jarl values your life immensely, and yet you don't strike me as one of noble birth.'

'I am not,' I admit, but also bristle slightly at that. 'All right.' I sigh. 'I am Kylan, Son of No One. My mother was from the Isle of Lewis in the Southern Isles, but we were taken in the raiding season many years ago.'

Why am I telling her this? But she doesn't laugh. Her eyes are on my hair.

Whatever our different stations in life, in that way we are the same.

She straightens up. 'I am Ingirid, Ragnvald's Daughter, heir to the Earl of Orkney. Call me Ingirid.' I stare at her, trying to absorb this information all over again. Then she stuns me by asking: 'So, can you play chess?'

The question is so ridiculous that I laugh out loud, before pretending a coughing fit to hide it. That starts me actually coughing, and I can't stop until the girl passes me a skin of water to drink from. 'I am a thrall.'

'Whatever you were before, you are a Jarl's companion now. You should learn some songs and poems, and stories too.'

Like the skald. I'd love that.

'Anyway, chess is the game everyone is playing now, you see? Here, we have all day. I have been told you will stay for another week, until the Archbishop is completely better. Next door they are trying all sorts of medicines on him. Meanwhile, let's have some fun, shall we? Can you play Hnefatafl? I need to know where to start.'

'Yes. I think I understand it.'

'Well, chess is a little like Hnefatafl, right? All figures are there to protect your king. See?'

She pulls a small table over and places a chequered game board on it. 'I know what the figures are,' I say, but when she reveals the gaming pieces, my face falls. Plain and ugly they are. 'This is the king,' she says, holding up a piece which could be anything, but has a cross carved into the top. 'Here is the queen…'

In my mind's eye I am back in the workshop, seeing the intricate and artistic figures we have created. *Where is the box with our chessmen now?*

Her pieces are made of wood—beech for the white and ebony for the black pieces. They are carved with skill; I can see it, but they aren't even a dull shadow of the treasure from our Trondheim workshop. She sets up the board with care. I watch pawns fill the second row from the edge. After that it gets confusing.

She laughs. 'Don't screw up your face like that, it's frightful! You'll soon learn. Rooks at each end, like this.' She places one on each corner. Then the knights and then the runners.'

'Bishops,' I mumble under my breath.

'What?'

'Nothing,' I hurriedly add, cursing myself for saying it

aloud. 'Sorry. I just let my mind wander, that's all.'

She gives me a long and searching look.

'What comes after the, erm, runners?'

She lifts the king and queen. 'White queen stays on a white square; black queen goes on the black square. Which leaves the king. *Voilà*!'

She drops the fashionable French word into the Norse language like a stone into soup and I look up, but her focus is on the game. She loves it, clearly. Her eyes are alive with sparkle as she explains each figure's moves to me, swatting my hand away whenever I attempt a forbidden move or don't wait my turn.

Tiredness soon pulls at my lids and the ache in my lungs reminds me of the fact that I am still ill. Nevertheless, her enthusiasm for this pastime is enough to keep both pain and fatigue at bay. The bell rings for vespers before she places her figures back into their polished box. 'You're quick to learn,' she whispers before slipping out through the door into the cold echoes of the hallway. 'We can continue tomorrow,' she calls over her shoulder.

I inhale deeply. She has been instructed to stay by my side and help me pass the time as my body banishes the curse in my blood. But almost as soon as I think that thought, I know it to be only half the truth. The other half, and it pains me to say it, is that she needs company too. She, too, needs to pass the time. If I can provide that service for her, however briefly, I'll be glad to do it.

It takes three more days for the fever to pass.

It takes five before I first beat her at chess.

It takes seven before I beat her every time we play.

17

ORPHIR

Orphir is a place of true beauty. In the fleeting moments when I am alone, I stretch my legs and look out over the glistening bay. The evening casts its amber light onto the roof of the round church as men gather for prayers. Twelve paces long, it must feel crowded with all of them in there. I find I can pray better up here in this chamber with the sound of the ocean whistling through the thatch and the call of the plovers by the shoreline.

Jarl Magnus has checked on me every day, but his countenance towards me has changed. There was warmth there before, as well as the reclusive air of a man with too many secrets to contain. But now, day by day, it increasingly seems as if an invisible wall has risen between us. Whenever I address him, he turns his face away. He finds excuse after excuse not to linger in my presence. It should not bother me, really—but now I feel I am a burden, a stone tied to his soul.

'Is he always like this?' Ingirid comments drily. 'What is wrong with him?'

'I don't know,' I answer truthfully, sliding my queen across the chessboard and replacing one of her pawns with it.

'How are you doing this?' She laughs and runs her ringed hand through her hair. It is then I see it.

'You are married?' My mouth falls open. I don't have much experience talking with women, or girls even.

'Yes. My husband is raiding Ireland, I think. My son—'

This time I really splutter out my drink. 'You have a son?'

'Yes, Elin. He is headstrong. He is being nursed in the south building. He is only little...'

Tears well up in her eyes and I wish I hadn't taken the pawn off her. Perhaps she is as much a slave as I am, trapped by wealth and status, separated from her son, abandoned by her husband.

'I think you may be well enough to join us for dinner this evening. The Archbishop is set to come down to the feasting hall for the first time since his affliction, too. Do come. I could do with some company nearer my own age.'

'I am a full five years younger at least.'

'I know. But look at us!' She points to her hair and mine. 'You could pass for my brother, could you not?'

I think about this. Truly she is not mistaken—we do look a little alike.

'I can't.'

'Why not? You have been placed in these chambers at your Jarl's request. Surely, he won't have any objections to your joining us?'

'Oh, I do declare he will!'

'For what reason?' By now, most of her hair has escaped from her headdress, rebel curls framing her blazing eyes.

I feel blood flush my cheeks and wonder why I still hold on to pride. *Why shouldn't I do as she asks? The truth is that I want to go to the feast. I wish I did belong under the soft blankets of a stately bed, that I deserved to drink from pewter goblets, instead of burnt earthenware.*

'By your silence, I understand you're coming?'

I let out something between a frustrated sigh and a groan.

'Excellent.' She smiles, crossing a diagonal step with one of her pawns to claim my queen.

'Check.' Her triumph oozes through every sound of her words.

I roll my eyes. I need to be more careful!

Later that evening, I wriggle into the linen shirt which has been left pressed over the seat by the bed and pull on the breeches left beneath. Whoever sent these clothes—

and it can only have been Ingirid—thought I was more hefty in body than I really am. Thankfully, there is string which runs through the waistband and I tie it as closely as possible.

Running the bone comb by the basin through my hair and fixing the clasp holding my upper garment in place, I stare at my reflection in the water, dull as it is. I barely recognise myself. My hair has grown long over my forehead, so I need to push it aside and tuck it behind my ear. There are crusty scratches across both of my cheeks and my face is paler than goats' milk.

The door creaks. 'Ready?'

I am not ready. When I thought of this plan of escape, I never imagined dining with an Earl. No, I merely thought of seeing the famed beaches of Lewis, and perchance hearing of my mother's fate. I can't even begin to think how I may bring all this about.

There is nothing for it. However longingly I stare at the overcoat with its familiar sea smell and Old Erik's tools concealed in the hem, tonight I must leave it behind.

I imagine I am a knight, bold and upright on horseback. Immediately, I feel the tension leave my spine and my shoulders slide backwards without my bidding. I grow an inch or two in height, and my eyes focus, with steady confidence. For all they know, I belong here. The more I tell myself that, the more I will believe it.

'Ready,' I answer, pushing open the door and stepping into the hallway of the Earl's Bu for the first time since I woke.

18

SVEN ASLEIFSSON

The hall is dimly lit, but candles illuminate the long wooden table and the platters of food thereon, and a roaring fire in the centre. Most of our oarsmen are already here, but all of them are wearing their own torn and threadbare shirts. I see a couple of them eye me with suspicion. There is Jarl Magnus, by the fireplace. Ingirid has gone to talk to one of the women by the vats of drink, so I begin to move towards him. 'Sir,' I begin, but he makes for the doorway.

So do I.

He speeds his steps.

So do I.

'Jarl Magnus, may I speak with you?'

A couple of people nearby turn their heads, and he halts, sighing, his face furrowed with impatience. He stares out into the darkness rather than face me. 'What is it now, boy? Have you need of anything else?'

I am taken aback. 'No, sir, I do not. Forgive me. I merely wanted to…'

And then I realise: I have no idea how to finish that sentence. I want to speak with him because I have come to depend on his counsel; his presence, however gruff, has become my day in and day out. He has not mistreated me. On the contrary.

'Why are you so displeased with me, Jarl Magnus?' My stomach contracts as if an actual blow had landed. 'Did I displease you?'

The Jarl is staring at me with bloodshot eyes. 'You, boy, saved my life out there at sea.'

'I'm sorry if I offended you, sir.'

'SILENCE!' he roars, and more than a handful of heads spin our way that time, despite the chatter and music and the choir of fire and wind.

He lowers his voice and draws near to my face. 'You see, boy, I am on a pilgrimage of penance. My mission is to atone, not to rack up a new debt.'

My head spins with all the words, unfamiliar, and said with such venom. 'I don't… I don't understand. Debt?'

'I owe you. As I owe many others. Believe me, there can be too much owing for a man to bear.' With this he swings his cloak around and marches towards the table, taking the seat of honour between the Earl of Orkney himself and the Archbishop who looks much recovered. The colour has returned to his cheeks. As soon as the Earl of Orkney sits, all the rest of the men sit too. Immediately opposite the host, a seat remains vacant. I clamber for a bench in the corner.

'Why are so many people here?' I whisper, mostly to myself, but Ingirid must have made her way back to me, her red wavy hair shining in the firelight.

'It's a farewell feast,' she states simply.

'For us? Are we to leave so soon?'

'I believe you are making ready,' she answers, 'But also—'

She never gets to finish her sentence, for there is a commotion at the door. A sturdy man of perhaps forty summers, with more scars than skin, pushes aside the door guard who stumbles backwards. He thrusts his shield aside and motions for thirty or forty more men to enter, all but sucking the light out of the place.

'Sven. You came.' The Earl of Orkney rises, and so do the Archbishop, and after a long few seconds' pause, Jarl Magnus. The newcomer walks through the crowd, which parts like molten butter, and thrusts himself down on the vacant seat opposite the host, clinking as he sits. *How many arms and weapons are concealed within his garments?*

I can barely feel Ingirid's breath on my neck as she whispers into my ear. 'Sven Asleifsson. Powerful local warrior. There are rival Earls of Orkney and Sven is yet to make up his mind who to side with. He is a merciless

Viking and a powerful friend to have, but a hard one to keep. Above all, he is a terrible, terrible enemy. I am worried. Father was hoping he'd come to the feast, but all those men. He's said to entertain a company of over eighty warriors at his Gairsay hall.'

I involuntarily take a step backwards and press my back against the cold stone of the wall. Conversation is stilted, even after a few drinks, but once the roasted hogs are brought in and the ale and meat loosen tongues, laughter fills all parts of the hall, including the centre where Ingirid's father, Earl Ragnvald Kali Kolsson sits. The only one whose body language differs is my own Jarl Magnus. When the Archbishop, still a little weakened from his illness, makes to retire, the Jarl rises and a shout rents the air. The Earl speaks.

'Norsemen! Countrymen! Thanes. We have gathered here to celebrate. It is a meeting of friends and allies. But it also celebrates my forthcoming voyage to the Holy Land on a Crusade.'

There is nodding from some quarters, but I am drawn to the faces of the Archbishop and Magnus. The Archbishop looks pleased and leads the applause by bouncing his drinking horn on the wooden table. As for Jarl Magnus, his face has drained of the last of its colour. Sven Asleifsson has risen too.

'Have a good journey, Ragnvald. May the powers of the Almighty protect you on your Crusade and may your raids on the way be profitable.'

Kolsson looks relieved. 'Can I count on your support? Your protection on my estate and my family?'

Asleifsson's scarred face contorts into a grimace, no doubt meant to be a smile.

'Oh, fear not, Ragnvald Kali Kolsson. My loyalty to the Earldom of Orkney cannot be in question, can it?'

Asleifsson's knuckles are white on the hilt of his sword, despite the semblance of friendship. Jarl Magnus answers with a grim stare. All around us, Sven's warriors stand ready to fight, too. But the moment has passed.

With a shrug, Asleifsson pushes past the assembled crowd, pausing for a moment to glare with greed at the Archbishop's fine clothes. He reaches the door and turns. 'As I say, I wish you a protected journey, Norsemen. May we be reunited soon.'

Something drips from his voice, but it is neither kindness nor goodwill. What it is, I cannot tell.

Ragnvald Kali Kolsson smiles. 'The same to you, my old friend. The same to you.'

The feast has lost its soul in some way. Magnus half-heartedly gnaws at his bone, the Earl attempts to joke and then offers a song, for he is a poet too. He even demands more drink to be brought, but one by one, his assembled court melts away.

'Withdraw if you wish.' Ingirid nods by the time the moon is high in the sky. 'Your Archbishop has just gone to bed, and you will set off in the next few days too.'

I walk off in the direction of my bedchamber, but only having done the walk once, I am suddenly unsure. By torchlight, all the corridors look the same. I wander along one, only to turn back when it leads to a kitchen still busy with thralls. Such as I used to be.

Retracing my steps, I breathe a sigh of relief when I hear a familiar voice, hushed but urgent. If the Jarl Magnus and the Archbishop are near, my chamber can't be far away. I creep towards them for fear of incurring their wrath.

'I am telling you, the man is as trustworthy as a hungry wolf! Lord Archbishop, I implore you, sail tomorrow, before he has time to organise his attack. I could sense it.'

'My dear Magnus, I am truly grateful for your counsel. But we must allow sufficient time to check over our ship. Leaving on the same day as Ragnvald Kali Kolsson may cause inconvenience to our hosts. Think again!'

'I have given this a great deal of thought, Archbishop. If you value your life, we must make ready at once.'

There is a pause, long and dark. I hold my breath. The subtle clinking sound of the Archbishop fingering his silver-studded robe echoes over the flagstones. Eventually he speaks.

'This is nothing but a hunch?'

Jarl Magnus sighs. 'This is *no less* than a hunch. These *hunches* have kept me alive. Hunches are prods of the

Almighty and we'd do well to act on them,' he breathes with suppressed rage, adding 'My Lord Archbishop' as an afterthought.

The Archbishop sighs. 'So be it. Make ready. We leave in the afternoon.'

'Can't it be morning?'

The Archbishop sounds truly irritated now. 'Morning. Fine. Eleventh hour.'

'Thank you, Archbishop. You won't regret it.'

With this, Magnus strides away from the Archbishop's quarters and right towards me.

RIGHT TOWARDS ME!

If he finds out that I've been eavesdropping, I'm done for! I slide behind a thick pillar and hold my breath once more.

Jarl Magnus turns the corner without dropping his stride and stops, suddenly. The sound of his sword, pulled slowly from his scabbard, scrapes through the air.

19

CURSES IN THE NIGHT

I stay still—pretending I am a gargoyle like the monsters which guard the façade outside. The corridor is silent now, apart from the rustling of the Archbishop's robes in his chambers, but I know that Magnus is there, unmoving, listening. His sword will be poised to strike at the merest hint of movement. A small noise, almost indistinguishable—he has taken the smallest of steps, silent as a cat. He means to walk around the pillar behind which I am hiding. *Which way is he going?*

I have to risk it. Barely breathing and with my upper body rigid as wood, for fear of jingling the decorative buttons, I move back. I hear the same small noise again, something between a creaking and a crunching—his boots were made for walking, for riding and feasting, not for sneaking silently in corridors.

I take another silent step back, praising the Almighty for the soft leather slippers I was given at the beginning of the night. I wish there was a light.

He has begun to walk away from me. Maybe he has simply decided that he is alone and has imagined the eavesdropper. Either way, he leaves me here, heaving for air, shaking with pent-up panic. It takes some moments before I trust my legs to carry me back towards my chamber.

The cloth covering my window flutters in the night breeze and I walk over to weigh it down with stones, when I hear something else.

Carefully drawing the curtains aside, I peek, just in time to see the candlelight go out in Jarl Magnus's chamber next door. But there is another light, to the left along the shore. Could the stories of faerie folk be true?

No. Faeries' voices are not coarse; they would not use Norse curses either. Who then?

The more I stare out, the more my eyes adjust to the shadows. There are man-shapes beyond the sea inlet—waving out to sea, at ships coming towards us, rigged and manned. I thank the Almighty for my sharp eyes: they bear the same mark as Sven Asleifsson's shield! *He only feigned his departure, and he has returned. Why?*

It does not take much imagination: the greed in his gaze was all too clear when he took in the Archbishop's appearance.

Treachery, of that I'm sure. The full moon lights the way, and if it disappears behind clouds, his signalmen on the beach do the work by waving a light.

I heard it all tonight. His fearsome reputation, such a scar-crossed face and the blood of so many Gaels and Irish on his hands.

What to do, what to do?

I think of the Earl of Orkney, and his Crusade. I think of Ingirid, left here defenceless, both a mother and a wife. I reach for my overcoat. *I must warn Magnus.*

He will know what to do!

20

THE PRECIOUS GIFTS

I grab Old Erik's overcoat and struggle into it as my feet slap down hard in the corridor. First, my fists fly against the door of the Archbishop's chamber, and then on that of Jarl Magnus. In a few hurried swipes, we claw together what can be salvaged. The man of God, already half-clad in his robes, makes for the door. *What urgency!* Jarl Magnus has set off to wake our men and to tell them to ready the ship. The hastily concocted plan is flawed, but it is the only one we have. We can get onto the ship, but we cannot hope to outsail Sven Asleifsson and his men. So we shall not try. Instead, we'll lie still in our sleeping bags on our ship, covered and out of sight. Sven's men will land. They will sneak off their ships to make for the Earl's Bu. Once they are in the building, we shall set sail under cover of darkness.

I don't know how Jarl Magnus thought of all of this so quickly, but glad of a plan, we agreed.

Now we are running along the corridor towards the stairs, the cloak of the Archbishop billowing in front of me. Waiting for us there is Jarl Magnus, his eyes grim and his teeth clenched, carrying a torch which he tries to conceal as he turns each corner. And then I remember.

'Oh, my Lord Archbishop! Your precious gifts! The wooden casket containing your beautiful chessmen!'

The Archbishop's eyes widen. 'They are concealed in a hidden cupboard beside the fireplace. I put them there myself as I didn't want to leave the valuables on the ship.'

'Leave them, boy. We'll be lucky to escape with our lives,' Magnus snarls, and the Archbishop gives a small sound of pain at the thought of losing his costly gifts.

'I'll go and get them.'

'You shall do no such thing, boy, you'll give us away and get us all killed.' But at this point, Magnus's voice ebbs away as I am too far gone already. Back up the stairs, back along the corridor, into the starlit chamber where the last dying embers glow in the fireplace. The cupboard lock is sealed! For a moment I am struck still. Who has the key? Have I risked my life in vain? I shall not accept that! I reach for the poker by the grate and wedge it into the crack. If I can get the angle right, I may be able to force it.

I wriggle and pray under my breath as time ticks away, imagining Sven Asleifsson and his crew splashing onto the beach below.

Crack. Finally, it gives. Like a lightning flash, I reach in and pull out the casket, so ornately carved and fit for a kingly gift. Tucking it under my arm, I sprint along the exit route, each step catapulting me closer to our people, our ship and to survival. Until I round the corner by Ingirid's chambers and stagger to a halt.

There is no time.

Don't even think about it.

Delay will mean certain death.

And yet, I stop, straighten my overcoat and knock.

At first I think she hasn't heard me at all. I am about to come to my senses and run when the door opens the tiniest of chinks and I see nothing but an eye, large with fear.

'Ingirid! It's only me.'

Her features relax and she unchains the door. 'What are you doing here, Kylan? Are you mad?'

'I had to warn you. Asleifsson is back. He means to raid the castle, I think, and he certainly means to capture our Archbishop. We are going to try to escape, but… but I couldn't go without saying goodbye. Or without saying thank you.'

Her eyes dart to the stairs and her gaze intensifies as she listens.

'Farewell. Thank you in return,' she finally breathes.

'And I had to show you these, ever so briefly.'

'What?'

'These!'

I flip open the lid of the casket and pull the topmost velvet pouch open. In the soft tallow candlelight, they look even more beautiful than before.

She gasps. 'These are… incredible. Chess pieces?'

I nod.

'The Archbishop's presents for the bishops and Lords of the Isles. How could I not show you after all you have taught me? But now I need to go.'

She lightly runs her hand across the delicately carved surfaces of the queens and the knights. Her voice is small when she speaks again.

'You have done me a kindness by showing me these. I am certain I shall never see the likes again. Be safe, Kylan No One's Son. My prayers will be with you.'

With that she closes her door and double and triple locks it; I can hear the clicks.

Pushing all other thoughts from my mind, I sprint down the stairs after my companions. Instead of using the front door, guarded by two of the Earl's men, I sneak out through the window of the hall downstairs. Judging by the dirty footprints on the windowsill, I am not the only one to have done that tonight. *Good, so they came this way.*

Our ship lies sea-ready, but it looks still and unoccupied. A little further down the shore, I can hear strange men talk in low voices. Murderous voices—full of ill intent. There is no sign of the Archbishop or Jarl Magnus, my moody companion. *They must be there.*

The problem is, if I run towards the boat, and am seen, I will lead the attackers straight to our hidden men. I also know that, as soon as Asleifsson and his Vikings are in the Earl's Bu, our ship will sail—whether I am on it or not. If I am abandoned here, even Ingirid's favour could not save me, of that I am sure. *What to do?*

I crouch low behind an upturned fishing boat to work out my chances. In the darkness, and with dread pounding in my veins, I map out an escape route. Asleifsson's men will march past this stretch of shore to the Bu again. I have only moments if I am to reach our ship before they come.

21

HAND OVER HOLD

I can make out ropes being thrown and tied on the shore nearby—the first of their ships are landing. *Now or never.*

Stooping low and darting from upturned boat to upturned boat, hiding behind coils of rope and empty barrels, I make for our ship. It looks godforsaken. But then I spot that all the sleeping bags are out on the deck, as they would be any night at sea. There is all but no movement. I can't rush into the water and splash towards the ship. That would attract attention. Instead, I abandon the heavy carved casket in the shallows and slip the velvet bags of gaming sets into my overcoat's hood. There is nothing for it but to wade in, careful to keep the ship between me and Asleifsson's men.

No wonder this man has built a reputation for stealth and brutality, and no wonder the northern seaboard lives in fear of him. From my wave-swept hiding place, I watch the two guards by the main door of the Bu fall without a sound. Still his men keep on coming, ten, twenty, thirty, fifty men—with axes and swords in their hands. It is a blessing that our oarsmen slept in the drinking hall, not far from the shore—it would have complicated things to fetch them from elsewhere. Now, however, I have another problem. If I want to remain unseen, I need to go deeper into the water. What if the chessmen get wet and soiled with seawater? I wade, feeling the cold brine burrow into my waist and chest, keeping as upright a posture as I can and standing on my tiptoes on the shifting seabed.

Finally, the last of Sven's warriors pass and I wonder whether to risk it when heavy steps on the gravelly beach alert me again. Two men only, but a shifting moonbeam illuminates one. It is Asleifsson himself, his scars appearing as deep gashes in the low light, distorted by sea-reflection. He raises his hand, as if to listen. Then he turns towards our ship, mumbling something to his companion. Silently, the men slink towards us. *What do I do? What do I do?* I consider holding my breath and dipping beneath the water, but I could only keep that up for a few seconds, and I would not be able to hear. Hearing and seeing—the double-stranded cord of survival. I take my chances and drop my chin into the water, pressing my head as close to the hull of our ship as possible. My teeth chatter too loudly, which is bound to give me away. On the deck of our galley, the men in their night sacks must hear them too. Asleifsson's companion's voice resumes with its low lilt: 'Do you think they have left valuables on the ship?'

Asleifsson scans our galley and shakes his head. 'No. The likes of the Archbishop would take the best loot inside to protect it from raiders. But there is something else we have to do.'

By this time, screams and metal-clanging noises have risen within the Bu's walls. Ingirid flashes through my mind. They would not hurt the Earl's daughter, surely? I cannot imagine they would harm her! But they may take her hostage because the Earl is a wealthy man! I am momentarily distracted by these thoughts—until I am brought sharply back to reality by the glint of something metal in Asleifsson's hand. He makes a noise, repulsive. It is chuckling. The man is amused!

My hand slips on the side of the ship—I need to work out how on earth I am going to get inside—the ladder is away. The rope is my only hope, the rope that yet tethers the vessel to land.

Asleifsson takes a step towards me. *Has he seen me?* He takes yet another step and raises his axe, so it is outlined in the moonlight, like a hellish angel of doom. Soon I won't be able to control my shivering. Something revolting has just brushed against my foot underwater—a jellyfish perhaps. I try to banish thoughts of more sinister creatures.

'We need to make sure that any fugitives of the bishop's party can't escape!'

Oh, have mercy on us, Lord Almighty He is going to damage our ship.

'Wait, Sven, best to cut the ship loose and let her drift into the bay. That way we can catch up with her later and add her to our fleet!'

'Just what I was thinking,' snarls Sven Asleifsson as if he had the idea first. His axe crashes onto the iron hook our ship is fastened to, sending a momentary spray of sparks into the night. Beside me, I feel the ship move as the first wave picks it up and begins to draw it out to sea. The two men on the beach laugh and begin to walk away, following their raiders to the palace.

The ship drifts to the right, revealing me for all to see, splaying in the sea and attempting to recover my balance. *The rope! I must not lose sight of the rope.*

Sieving through the muddy brine with my fingers, I touch it twice but cannot get a purchase. I MUST get hold of the rope. Eventually, I close my fist around it and only just in time—the ship gives a powerful jerk and I am torn off my feet and dragged into the depths. And now my hood with its chessmen cargo becomes a deathly stranglehold on my neck.

I can barely breathe.

Wrong. I cannot breathe at all.

Out of the corner of my eye, I see what has caused the

sudden forward movement—someone has set sail on our ship. At the very same time, there is a roar of anger on the beach, and a spear flies past my head, grazing my ear, and impaling itself into the wood of our ship. Water pounds my face and I struggle to heave air into my lungs, never mind see, or shout for help. For all I know, here I am going to hang until my strength gives way and I drop into the ocean, sinking without a trace, and the chess pieces with me. Our men do not know to look for me.

I nearly lose my hold on the rope when it is pulled upwards, roughly, momentarily loosening my hood's stranglehold. 'It is me!' I scream in my death-fear. How thoughts of Stoorworms and Krakens form in my mind at a time like this, I do not know, but they do. 'Help! Jarl Magnus! Lord Archbishop. I am here! Help me!'

A large amount of salty black brine sweeps into my mouth as I scream, cough, swallow and gag. I have little strength. They won't hear me in their industry to get away, shooting their own arrows at the enemies on the shore, who are bound to sail after them as fast as their own ships allow. *One hand above the other. Up and up and up.* I strain and pull, strain and pull. Sea salt rubs into my raw skin and stings me awake. My upper body is clear of the water now, with the gaming pieces still weighing me down at the back. Strength returns to my arms which have lifted so many blocks of wood, buckets and tusks. I think of each contour I carved into the chessmen. *Hand over hold, hand over hold.* My feet close around the rope and find a foothold against the spear in the rump of the ship. *Hand over hold.* An arrow flies from the railing, just above my head. 'I am here! Don't shoot!' I try to shout it, and yet it comes out like a pathetic whimper. *Hand over hold, pull.* The top of my head will be visible over the edge of the gunwale. They may think I am one of Asleifsson's men and kill me with a single blow, or they may help me in. Both are preferable to this.

There are shouts from inside the ship, calls of genuine distress.

I hear Jarl Magnus's voice above all.

'Halt! It's the redhead!'

22

A TROUBLED SOUL

Everything happens lightning-fast after that. Strong arms reach over the gunwale and haul me over. By now my body is so cold that I can't even feel the scrapes of wood over my bare legs where my breeches have torn. Hot blood, stinging brine, the groaning and grunting of men rowing for their lives, as Asleifsson and his retinue fade further and further away on the beach. I thought they would pursue us with their ships, but Asleifsson is too experienced to chase a lost cause. We escaped, right under his nose. His roar of anger will linger in my memory for a long time to come.

With the Archbishop back in his private cabin below deck, the men get to work on the oars. I shed my dripping overcoat and Jarl Magnus hands me a dry blanket. In the east, the sky lightens with promise. The sail billows in the wind and I anxiously squint to see if Asleifsson has chosen to burn the Earl's palace down, but no. In the far, far distance, his ships seem to make their way back towards his seat at Gairsay in the east and I breathe a sigh of relief for Ingirid and her people.

'His quarrel is not with the Earl Ragnvald,' Magnus growls beside me. 'His quarrel is not even with us. Men like Asleifsson need riches and power. His reputation is built on looting and slaughter. Now even he cannot escape that.'

'Would he want to?' I ask.

The Jarl stares into the distance. 'No.'

I struggle to equate it all. The raiding and the murdering and the looting, accompanied by prayers and chapel-visits in between drinking sessions.

'Do not trouble yourself. He will have found the casket in the Archbishop's chamber, I'm sure.'

A shiver runs down my spine. *Of course! The chessmen!*

'They are not lost, sir. The gaming pieces, I mean.'

Confusion twists his face. 'What do you mean?'

'Look. The hood of my garment yonder. There.'

I stumble across the deck to lift it and yes, to my intense relief, the sodden hood is still weighted down by its valuable load.

I wrestle the velvet pouches out of the garment and present them, dripping, to Jarl Magnus who stares at me in wonder. 'You risked your life to retrieve them?'

It sounds sort of heroic when he puts it like that.

'I suppose,' I mumble and glance sideways.

His glare intensifies as wisps of dark hair blow across his face. 'I cannot figure you out, boy,' he finally mutters and rises to assess our ship's course.

'And I cannot you,' I answer in a whisper, to no one but myself. It is true. *What is a man like him doing in the service of the Archbishop? How does a man like him know so much about Sven Asleifsson? And why, for all his strength and warrior-courage, is he the most troubled soul I have come cross in my young life?*

The sun is high in the sky. The men are muttering about something they call a whirlpool in the sea where, according to the old religion, the gods selected their sacrifices. They say that even the bravest of soldiers and sailors become powerless there.

I'm strangely unaffected. I cannot change whether we live or die, and whether we reach the Southern Isles or whether we do not. But I spend a very happy hour checking every single figure of the chess sets for sea damage. A little water has found its way into the pouches, but it is as nothing, considering what the damage could have been. Even the crimson dye on some of the figures is still flawless. As I line them up in the correct order on the deck, heavy footsteps approach and Jarl Magnus's huge hulk bears down on me once again. I know he means me no harm, but I flinch nonetheless. Old habits die hard.

'You know how to arrange figures for chess?'

The boat rocks in the waves and my hand hovers to steady the figures. 'A little, sir,' I offer, shrugging.

He gathers the figures back into their wool-lined pouches which have been drying on the sail-rope. 'I'll take these down to the Archbishop. Go on, make yourself useful.'

I rise and stumble towards the crates of supplies at the back of the ship. There are two skins of fresh water which I proceed to share out between the rowers. Beads of sweat pearl off their foreheads, and they stare left more than once. The whirlpool.

'Hold your course, men!' Magnus yells before he disappears into the Archbishop's domain. 'Hold your course.'

The tillerman hollers back: 'If only it was that easy!'

23

THE SEA WITCH'S WHEEL

Going without sleep is not wise, however necessary it may have been. Minds wander, eyelids droop. The wind can play its tricks, spinning ships like ours backwards into a giant vortex in the Pentland Firth when they should be sailing safely around Cape Wrath and heading for the Isle of Lewis.

'Down with the sail,' Jarl Magnus roars. 'Down! Down!'

A particularly strong gust of wind catapults us sideways and now I see it too—the sea, curling its watery lip as if sneering at us in our peril. It may be daylight now, but the grey clouds above us churn, just as the sea below us does. Still shivering, I sink down against the gunwale.

Live? Die? I care not. If the Almighty pleases to steer us so, what point is there in resisting? And as I knock on St Peter's Gate of Heaven, I will have an Archbishop for company. My chances of passing through have never been better.

'Ow!' I croak rather than shout as my voice nearly gives out. I lie sprawled at the Jarl Magnus's feet. His kick has certainly roused me from my morose thoughts.

'Get up.'

He is tightening a rope to stop our sail from fluttering and tearing. He looks down at me again. 'Get up! I didn't save you for failing. I saved you to succeed. We're not done on this earth yet, not you and not me!'

I am not sure I agree with him. The boat has moved in a wide semi-circle on the sea's surface—I can tell by the sun's position over the ship. We are already in the outer vortex of the whirlpool. *God help us all!* The lip of water, risen from the surface, bubbles as if to put a spell on us. The fear takes hold of them all, I can feel it. Our oarsmen strain. Magnus shoves me towards one of them with his shoulder, struggling to retain the rope. 'There!'

Now I see it—the oarsman has slumped on his seat—he has fainted. With an actual mission, my resolve returns too: here is something to do. I quickly lower the man onto the deck of the ship where brine sloshes around his motionless body. No, there, his face twitches, he is coming to. But there is no time to waste. With barely a second to spare, I prevent his oar from sliding out of its hook and into the sea. Pushing with my whole body, I jerk a little until I discover the rhythm of the other rowers. Forward, down, backwards, pull, upwards and forward again. The Caller's instructions are clear and, once I have become part of the movement, I feel that I am doing something. And it does me good.

Jarl Magnus gives me a brief, satisfied nod before his attention is taken up with the sail again. Is it me or is the hungry lip of water further away than it was?

My body *becomes* my movement. My mind hovers somewhere in the air above my head as I rise and fall, push and pull, in a choreographed dance with the man in front and the man behind. I may be small and scrawny by comparison, but my muscles ripple under my torn garment and, strangely, I have never felt so alive. There is the joy of escape, the joy of movement, the joy of fresh air and wind and sea.

Eventually, the drum sounds and with a groan, all of us sink back in our seats and allow the oars to slide into their resting hooks.

'The Swallower,' Magnus comments drily.

'The what?' The question is out of my mouth before I can consider its wisdom.

'The Swelkie, to give it its proper name. It's what they call the whirlpool. Others refer to it as the Sea Witch's Wheel. We have had two narrow escapes in as many days.'

I crane my neck and look backwards. Right enough, behind us in the distance, the surface of the sea is still behaving strangely.

'A whirlpool is nothing to do with witches,' the Jarl

snarls dismissively. 'This vortex is caused by the fastest currents I've seen anywhere in the world—and I have sailed to many places. Treacherous, this route, but the quickest way to the Southern Isles.' With that, my companion turns and makes for the Archbishop who has emerged from his chamber. Pale and exhausted he looks, but healthy. Come to think of it, I too feel that my strength is restored.

Sometime later that evening, having rowed hard past the rocky cliffs of a place they call Cape Wrath, I crawl into a damp sleeping bag, in my damp clothes, and long for the fires in the Earl's Bu again. Suddenly, a blanket lands on me and I raise my head to see. The Jarl Magnus. I lift a hand in thanks and wrap the warm cloth around my upper body.

Under his breath, the oarsman beside me spits sideways. 'The favoured one, and a thrall!' he snorts. Grumbles of dissatisfaction start from three or four men nearby. *The Jarl's favour on me is making the others jealous. Why did I not think on this before?*

Slowly, I open my eyes a chink and peer carefully into the darkness. Just as I dreaded, eyes have come to rest on me. Hostile eyes. Envious eyes. Men who have again and again risked their lives for the Archbishop and his mission, and who feel passed over and ignored for the sake of a slave boy.

Oh, Almighty Lord, I must be careful.

As if had just occurred to me, I take the blanket and throw it to the man beside me. 'I don't need it,' I say, already looking away. 'I'm warm enough. You have it.'

It is something. But will it be enough?

Only time will tell.

At first light, we hoist the sail, and with favourable winds, speed out towards the islands and the Minch. Majestic golden beaches sing in the light, and the landmass we approach, I am told, is the Isle of Lewis. I may have been here before, but I do not remember it.

Settlements along this seaboard are sparse and windswept. Rounding the island on its western side, we pass two glorious beaches, one small and one bigger, and each time I wonder if this is where we will land. But Jarl Magnus looks southwards, pointing out landmarks. The Archbishop seems very interested in an old broch of magnificent height, soon followed by a circle of standing stones not unlike the ones we saw in Orkney, but far, far in the distance. A deep slash of sea into the land follows and we bear right again. I have studiously avoided Jarl Magnus's company, but now I cannot help myself. I am drawn to his tales of the Lords of the Isles. I might as well admit it: I am attracted to tales like a bear to honey. He is in deep conversation with the Archbishop.

'This is the seat of the Lords of the Isle of Lewis, the peninsula called Bernera, crowned by these most magnificent sands. I believe this place to be Bosta. Let's beach the ship here, Archbishop. But one word of caution: it would be wise to approach the seat of the Lords with care. In these lands, friends or foes change with the wind.'

24

LORD LJOTOLF'S LANDS

No Norse gravel on these shores, oh no. As far as the eye can see, there is golden beach—as if gilded by heaven. It is windy though, with each gust lifting the top layer of sand and sweeping it landwards like sorcery.

Jarl Magnus pulls the ship forward as he splashes into the surf and motions to the men to do the same. 'Here, give me a hand.' Soon, all of us are knee-deep in the low waters, but these shallows have been warmed by the sun and are clear as daylight. In the glinting rays, I observe the tiniest of fish dart around my breeches.

'And UP!' the Jarl yells. We pull the galley clear of the waterline. The Archbishop is helped out and kneels by the clear blue sea, offering thanks for provision and protection. We all stand beside him, mumble our responses and make the sign of the cross. When the man of God stops speaking, Jarl Magnus raises his voice. 'And now, be vigilant. Our ship will not have gone unnoticed.

We are sure to be greeted, with good or ill intent.'

I swallow. Out of the corner of my eye, I observe movement between the dunes. A little girl in a dark dress. An old man aided in his hobbling walk by a wooden crutch. The closer I look, the more the hills are alive with movement and colour. Raiders often pass these shores. They will look at us with suspicion, make no mistake. But no one moves to harm us or confront us.

Oh.

It would appear I spoke too soon.

Thirty or so warriors are pouring down the hillside, encircling us as they spread out. Their swords are drawn, so we raise our weapons too. And yet there is something half-hearted about the confrontation, as if all of us were just actors in a saga play, feigning heroic actions without meaning them ourselves.

'*Heilir.* What brings you here?'

The greeting, delivered with aggression despite wishing us health, is in Norse, not Gaelic. These are Norsemen! Jarl Magnus raises his sword high above his head and looks the leader in the eye. Then he lets his weapon thud into the sand where it bounces and lies still. 'We mean you no harm. We bring you a great blessing. The messenger of the Almighty stands among you. His Highness, the Archbishop of Nidaros.'

The Lewismen exchange glances, and I detect their wish to laugh, the urge to stare in disbelief. But now the

Archbishop himself walks forward in the crowd. Despite our hasty departure from Orkney, he cuts an impressive figure with his velveteen cloak, his carved crozier and his calm gaze.

The leader of the group looks round, maybe seeking guidance from his men.

'Pray, take me to the Lord of these shores,' the Archbishop insists. 'You won't regret it.' With this, all our remaining men sheath their swords and tuck their axes back into their belts.

The leader of the group gives something between a bow and a kneel, a strange gesture. 'Very well,' he offers.

We walk, flanked by Lewismen on both sides. A drinking hall soon comes into view, rectangular and stone-built, with a magnificent carved dragon head at its gable on both sides. Thatched with thick marram grass, 'tis a sight to behold. Not far from it is a farmstead, with fenced land and huts clustered around it. Four full-size ships lie by the shore, an instant sign of wealth indeed—and of intent to raid.

I fear them.

The wily Archbishop sidles up to the leader of the group, speaking in a low voice. 'We are but strangers to these shores. Pray, tell us a little more about those who rule so powerfully here. Who commands the respect of such fine men as yourself?' I see the brief flash of silver pass from the Archbishop's hand into that of the leader.

With a jingle, the man slides it into the purse dangling from his belt and straightens his overcoat. 'The Lord of these lands is Ljotolf, a Norseman who rules at Bosta. To the south, he has quarrels with an emerging warlord and a Gael by the name of Somerled, but our hold on Lewis is firm.' The Archbishop nods his head. Jarl Magnus is walking ahead of the group, but no doubt he heard every word.

He is not looking our way, and that in itself makes me suspicious. He marches on, head down, but I thought I detected a twitch at the name Ljotolf. Could they have met before? Or does he know something about this Ljotolf that the rest of us do not?

Sweat begins to form on my neck and spine. Jarl Magnus keeps his head down, all the way to the great hall which is almost as impressive as the Earl of Orkney's. Inside stands a broad, bearded man with browning teeth and a high-held chin.

'An Archbishop, eh?' he sneers.

We all flinch, even the man of God who surely wishes to portray an air of authority. He recovers quickly though.

'*Heill*, Lord Ljotolf.' The Archbishop inclines his head in a polite gesture of recognition, but the bearded, unkempt man in front of him reeks of ale and slaps the bishop on the shoulder so hard that he all but loses his balance. Jarl Magnus's hand hovers over his sword hilt, a fact not lost on Ljotolf's retinue who do the same.

'Just being friendly!' guffaws the Lord of Lewis until the laughter turns to coughing. He pats his stomach. 'You are thrice welcome. How did you break your journey? I cannot imagine you sailed from Norway in one, did you?' He walks forward, scanning each of the faces in turn. Normally, Jarl Magnus would speak on behalf of the Archbishop, but for some reason he stays silent, the collar of his garment turned up high. Ljotolf stops in front of me.

'Tell me, young one, what's a boy doing on a ship like this? You look a bit wet behind the ears, do you not? If there's an oar bench set aside for weaklings, what does that say about the state of Nidaros?' He laughs again.

I bristle and speak in a clear voice. 'With respect, Lord Ljotolf, I am not a weakling. I only seek to serve the Lord Archbishop. I have some Gaelic and hope to be of use with the Gaelic chieftains.'

'Ahh,' he leans down, his rough nose almost level with my eyes. 'You can try your Gaelic on young Lord Somerled, troublesome beggar that he is! But for now, you are here, and as luck would have it, I am expecting further company soon. He is someone I'd like you to meet, young one. He can teach you all there is to know about being a Viking: seafaring and raiding! My oldest friend, Sven Asleifsson is expected here on the island any day now! He stops by on his summer raiding trips to

Ireland. I cannot imagine what has delayed him.'

He guffaws loudly again as a bubble of dread forms in my stomach.

25

VESPERS

I watch as eyes of steel shoot up from under Jarl Magnus's hood, casting about the room, assessing escape routes. But the Archbishop calmly states: 'We should be delighted to meet your friends and count them our own. For now, though, do you have a chapel in which I could conduct mass for my men? It is time for vespers. After that, perhaps my thrall boy could be escorted to my quarters with my things?'

Some of our oarsmen snigger. They enjoy me being put in my place as a slave, I suspect. My heart, however, skips a beat. *I am here, finally, on the Isle of Lewis, just as I prayed.*

In the Norse tradition, the chapel is little more than a cellar down some stone steps into the ground from the drinking hall. I watch the men disappear downwards, with little option but to play along. There are whispers and questions. Soon, the clear voice of Archbishop

Jon Birgersson rings out, joined somewhat reluctantly by oarsmen and warriors, who are much more used to rowing and swinging a sword than saying prayers.

Jarl Magnus checks carefully over his shoulder. None of Ljotolf's guards have followed us down. Lord Ljotolf seems to have business with his men just now. Being nearest the stairs, I could sneak back to listen what they say, but I cannot think how, without arousing suspicion.

With a meaningful look, the Archbishop starts the opening prayer, speaking so loudly that those upstairs can't help but hear. He motions for our men to join in, and they do—voices rough and unpractised in such refined Latin. Jarl Magnus joins in with gusto, allowing the Archbishop to step closer and whisper in his ear. The Archbishop sings again, with the Jarl leaning over to give him his answer. Again, Jarl Magnus picks up the tune, accompanied by our half-hearted oarsmen. The bishop whispers to him urgently once more.

I can't do anything but sing; sing to provide cover for their conferring, and for what has to happen next. When the melody nears its end, the Archbishop sinks to his knees and all of us follow his example.

The cold stone slabs on the ground spread their dread into my heart. *The very villain who made us flee Orkney is on our trail. What's worse, the local Lord will welcome him with open arms, as the best of friends!*

The Archbishop begins another loud prayer, giving

thanks for our safe passage and the magnanimous welcome here, no doubt for the benefit of anyone who might listen in. Meanwhile, Jarl Magnus has tiptoed halfway up the stairs. He returns with a nod, signalling that the coast is clear. Without breaking his flow and in exactly the same sing-songy voice, the Archbishop continues: 'We will attend the feast tonight. Before it, I will speak with our host Ljotolf and explain, asking him to speak for a settlement between ourselves and Sven Asleifsson. Each of you, conceal a dagger in your boots on the way to the feast, in case things should get out of hand. Now may the Lord bless you and keep you, in spiritu sanctu…'

'*Amen*' the men all echo, singing out their relief. There is a strategy, and they know what it is.

We traipse back up the stone stairs and I reflect on how easy it would be to trap an enemy down there in the chapel. A few burning torches would do the job. I follow the Archbishop who turns and waves me on. Lord Ljotolf is seated in the midst of his warlords. From the little snippets I pick up, he is planning a raiding trip later this summer and needs another ship. They speak a mix of Norse and Gaelic.

The Archbishop clears his throat. 'This is my thrall boy. Would you show him to my quarters now, please? He will carry my luggage and belongings.'

I hoist the heavy roll of cloaks upon my shoulder and

stagger a little before lifting the Archbishop's private copper box. The gentle clinking and shifting of weight alert me. *Of course, without the casket, the chessmen needed new protection and he has hidden them inside this simple box.*

I take good care not to drop it. Five sets of ivory chessmen create some weight, and I don't want that guard to know what I am carrying! A treasure like this is worth cutting ten thrall boys' throats, and without a second thought.

The guard struggles ahead of me with the Archbishop's travel chest. Lord Ljotolf's hall is great, but the residence beside it does not lack splendour or comfort either. The stairs lead up into a rounded quarter beyond which we pass into an adjacent chamber. A wooden slat and thick bog cotton mattress lie on a plinth. A jug of water sits beside and a fire crackles on the hearth, feeding its smoke out through the roof thatch.

Now is the moment. Now is the time. I always knew that the point would come when I would have to set out alone.

'This will do,' I say searching for as much authority as I can muster in my voice. It seems to fool the man who led me here. *How much a proper overcoat and an embroidered shirt can belie one's status!* 'Go,' I command, louder. To my astonishment, he does.

I wait and listen. The noblemen are engaged in a

conversation about hounds below stairs.

This is my chance.

I eye the copper box.

26

THE CHESSMEN THIEF

I have to run away. Deep down, I have always known it would come to this, haven't I? But if I escape, how am I to pay my way?

I already know the answer. Cold sweat forms at the back of my neck.

I stretch a shaking hand out towards the copper box and its treasures, but my conscience constricts my throat and tightens my chest.

It is a sin to steal.

But without any kind of wealth, I am doomed. A free man needs silver, or ways to obtain it. And my hands helped fashion the chessmen. They are as much mine as the Archbishop's.

I choose to believe the lie and blind myself to the truth. Maybe freedom *and* a clear conscience are too much to ask. I cannot choose both.

And here, in Lord Ljotolf's dwelling, I choose

freedom. Forcing a step towards the chessmen, I strain my ears, eyes and heart.

Quickly. If I do not act now, I will remain a slave.

Resolute, I grasp the copper box and open it. There they lie, encased in velvet cloth pouches and cushioned by finely spun wool. How far we have come, these pieces and I, all the way from Trondheim.

I empty my mind of thought, now that I am committed. Looking over my shoulder, I hurriedly empty the figures from their pouches, with no care for size and shape, or even for complete sets. I rake in some of the tables-men too and let them jumble into the folds of my tunic and overcoat. I'll hide them better when an opportunity presents itself. For now, I need to get out of here. As an afterthought, I reach into my own bundle and shake out a handful of pebbles from the beach for games of Hnefatafl with the oarsmen. Now the stones can help me not to not arouse suspicion. Carefully, I tip them into the velvet pouches and place them in the copper box before closing the lid.

Oh no, footsteps!

Panicking, I slip the box under the Archbishop's garments and just manage to recover my balance before any of the chess pieces spill onto the stone-cold floor from my tunic.

'What are you doing?' comes a voice, icy and harsh, from the open doorway.

'Hanging the Archbishop's robes so they can straighten,' I reply, struggling with the long fabric to make my words believable.

Jarl Magnus raises a single eyebrow.

I do not move now, for fear that a chessman may spill from my pocket as I crouch, or from my hood as I bend. In fact, I worry that a single breath will result in my exposure. *He knows. Surely, he knows.*

Never taking his eyes off me, he strides towards the Archbishop's bed. Still staring, he pushes the pile of clothes aside to reveal the copper box.

He lifts it and, very deliberately, weighs it in his hand. His eyes remain on me.

My conscience splinters into a million pieces. If I open my mouth, I'll surely confess all, so I bite down on my lip and focus at the wall. He is no fool, but it appears that he is not so very attentive either. He flips the lid open.

I don't know what he expected, but the box is not empty. That seems enough for him and he does not investigate past the velvet covers. Eyeing his sword hanging by his side, I wonder how long it would be before he'd run me through, if only he knew what is weighing down every fold of my overcoat. Once more, he balances the copper box on the palm of his hand and weighs it carefully.

He breaks into a broad smile. 'You had me there!' he laughs and I force myself to laugh along, casting my eyes down at the floor in case they give me away as the mirrors of my soul. He replaces the box on the Archbishop's bed. 'You really had me, boy! For a moment, I thought that, after all of this time, you were going to turn thief and run!' His laugh grows deeper and I manage a fairly convincing giggle. As I hoped, he moves on.

'You're sleeping in the stables this time. No luxury treatment now, I'm afraid. But there are blankets laid out for you, I'm told, and as long as you serve drinks alongside Lord Ljotolf's servants, you are welcome at the feast too. At sundown in the hall.'

There is a sawing at my heart, up and down, deeper and deeper. This man has risked his life for me, and I for him. I'm sure neither of us have the first idea why. It just happened.

'Why so nervous?' he smiles, still chuckling. 'Go! We'll meet at sundown.'

I am fearful to move at all with my precious hidden cargo. Thankfully, he misinterprets my slowness. 'And don't worry too much about Sven Asleifsson. We are already under his friend's protection. It's unlikely he will risk any slaughter under Lord Ljotolf's roof, however tempting the loot.'

'But wouldn't the Archbishop fetch a handsome ransom? If he was captured?'

Jarl Magnus carefully tucks his dagger into his sock and rolls his breeches down again. 'These journeys are always risky. The Archbishop knew that. If he is killed, or goes missing, they'll simply appoint another.'

'And if your thrall goes missing, you'll appoint another?'

I want to cut off my tongue for saying this. A quick glance up and a shadow passes over his face, briefly.

'You're right. We're all of us replaceable.' With that, he turns to the window and I am dismissed. Light on my feet, I attempt to glide out through the open doorway, but my laden hood catches on the corner, giving a telltale click and jingle. *Has he heard?* I cough violently to mask the sound as I tug it free and, the Lord be thanked, it doesn't tear. But there is no getting away from it now, no question at all.

I am a thief and I have made my bed.

Now I must lie in it.

27

TO THE STANDING STONES OF CALLANISH

It is so much colder than it used to be, with the sharp wind biting into every flap of my garment and tearing at my breeches. All I can hope for is to make my way east along the shore towards some sort of settlement. Perhaps I will find a boat, or a path. Perhaps not. Perhaps I will find my mother before the bell tolls for me. Perhaps not. But one thing is certain: if I have a hope of finding her, this island is where she will be.

I try to remember what she looked like, but memory is fickle, is it not? Hair the colour of flame and ashes, of that I am certain. A light complexion with a dusting of freckles, and a smile which conquered her eyes every time she laughed. But I remember the sadness, too. Her helplessness as she watched Gunnar and Einar lead me away to the workshop. The pain of farewell as she was forbidden to see me and I her. I was old enough, they said. No seven-year-old should need his mother anymore. Thralls should work; it was their destiny and their calling. "*Your destiny was a free man's once*" she whispered in my ear. 'The Southern Isles are your home, The Isle of Lewis. Remember this all your life, Kylan.'

Here I am, in the midsummer drizzle with nothing but a stolen leather stable-sack of priceless treasure, but at least I can move again. I thought about sneaking into the feast first and taking some supplies, but my heart was already too full of remorse. Besides, if Sven Asleifsson does come, or if the Archbishop looks for the gifts which I have now stolen from him, what hope have I of survival?

I know very well that in either case, I will have none.

My chances here, out in the open, may be small, but they are better. Resolutely, I stride towards a small coracle lying by the waterside and push it into the sea, jumping in. I saw the standing stones in an inlet east of here. There is bound to be a settlement that way. With luck, I'll find help there. I begin to paddle east, hugging the coast, through a narrow sea passage. Then I turn south where I can make out the distant silhouettes of the standing stones. My arms begin to ache.

Lord Ljotolf's house must be making ready for the feast. My absence will have been discovered by now.

Not long after I hear voices. At first, they are distant and intermittent. I scan the land on either side for pursuers, but to my dismay, the threat comes from four, nay five, skiffs, gaining on me on the water.

An ungodly word crosses my lips.

Given the fact that I am carrying riches worth more than a nobleman's estate, I am not surprised at their urgency. I double the speed of my paddling. The standing stones on the hillside ahead are much closer now. The tide is on my side, carrying me in towards the shore much faster than I could row myself. As soon as the water is knee-deep, I splash to shore.

'THERE! There he is! The reward is mine; I saw him first!'

Another gruffer voice joins him. 'The reward goes to the one who retrieves the treasure. My knife will get to the boy before yours.'

Behind me, the first of my pursuers' boats runs aground in the shallows.

And I clutch the bag of chessmen to my chest and run up the hill towards the ancient stones. I have no weapons. Even if I had, resistance would be futile. But there is an inbuilt instinct to risk anything—yes, anything—to breathe but a moment longer and to sing another night. I don't know where the energy comes from but come it does.

Forward, is all I can think. *Nearly there.* I stumble on the uneven ground, just as two axes whistle above my head and embed themselves in the ground a little way off. With a groan, I pull myself up again, my hands clawing through moist moss and clumps of grass. A spear bounces off the first standing stone as I reach the monument. Using the large monoliths for cover as I weave in and out, I reach the inner circle.

I am spent.

Shaking the sack off, I sink against the tallest slab at the centre, breathe deeply and allow my lids to close, despite the approaching footsteps. It is over.

The next instant, I am jerked upright and a sword glides against my throat. Another pierces into my back. As my eyes focus, I stare in turn into the faces of Jarl Magnus and—my stomach rents—Sven Asleifsson.

Behind those two, approximately thirty men at arms stand among the stones, axes hanging from their belts, daggers clutched in their fists.

28

POWER AND FURY

The faces. It is the faces which haunt me the most. Asleifsson is all sneer, amusement and bloodlust. Jarl Magnus, on the other hand is stern and cool. But I have learned to read him like a scholar reads a rune. Behind that mask is nothing but disappointment. Bitter disappointment in who I have revealed myself to be. I'm ashamed. Not of being a thrall, but of behaving like one.

Would freedom ever have been in my grasp? Perhaps. Perhaps I could have earned it, with a champion like Jarl Magnus by my side.

But now, by running, I have condemned myself to death—or a lifetime of slavery if I am lucky.

Asleifsson steps back and raises his sword hand. 'He's yours to run through, Magnus. Then let's take the bag and get back to the feast.'

It's a challenge, delivered with a leer. In the dimming light, the Viking's helmet, his scars and his darkened teeth are more shadow than shape. I swallow and try to remember some of my prayers. If only Jarl Magnus wouldn't stare at me like this. *Look away. Please look away!*

But he doesn't. His eyes rest on me, wondering, weighing up options. And then he decides. 'We'll take him back to the feast. Lord Ljotolf will want to have his sport with the boy first. And the men like a diversion in the midst of the feasting.'

There is a mumble of assent from the gathered warriors.

Am I to die in front of them all? An audience fit for a traitor and a liar and a thief. I hang my head.

'Aren't you going to speak?' Jarl Magnus asks, authority in his voice. Asleifsson is watching him closely.

I grit my teeth. I know what he wants. An explanation, a reason, a justification for my failure. But I cannot give it, least of all to him.

'Doesn't look like it. We could put it beyond all doubt by cutting his tongue out.' Sven Asleifsson's suggestion is met by laughter from his men. Someone is scraping the blade of a knife across his shield and I shudder, much to the men's amusement. I feel myself pushed and we set off. My shoulder feels oddly light now, relieved of the leather bag with all the chessmen. Jarl Magnus has tied it to his belt.

My mind shuts down, readying itself for the suffering

that is sure to come—and for an eternity of judgement thereafter. I shall never see my mother again. I shall never see another sunrise. My journey has been in vain, and strangely, this only produces a dull sort of sadness. There is no rage and no fight left in me.

For the short sail back to Bosta, I lift my chin and fix my gaze on the sunset. All too soon, the dragons of the drinking hall come into view. Fragments of music and laughter drift over to us in the air. With each step and each shove, I am reminded of my place. *Bear it, endure it, do not disgrace your name further. Show valour and courage till the end.* At least I am blessed to have seen this island again before I die.

'In there.'

Golden fire-glow emanates from the drinking hall's doorway. Behind us the golden beach still glows, even in the dusk that surrounds it. Flecks and wisps of light still scrape across the sky.

Jarl Magnus does not look back as he leads the way and Sven Asleifsson stays close behind me. As soon as we enter the hall, the chatter falls silent. There he is, Lord Ljotolf, flanked by the Archbishop. The churchman's eyes fall on me then swivel to the leather bag dangling from my companion's belt. He casts his eyes down. I hope he remembers that it was I who warned him back in Orkney.

I glance at Sven whose greedy eyes already strip the

Archbishop of his fine garments. There is no doubt: the only reason there is a peaceful agreement for now is that both of our parties are on friendly terms with Lord Ljotolf, nothing more. As soon as Sven Asleifsson and Lord Ljotolf can confer privately, no one's life will be safe.

Not that it matters for me. A final rough push from behind, and I am sprawled across the floor before the island nobleman. I stay as still as possible, but Jarl Magnus steps over me with care, delivering the chessmen bag back into the hands of the Archbishop. 'Here, Lord Archbishop. As far as I can tell, your gifts are safe.'

'Boy,' Lord Ljotolf rasps with a mixture of rage and glee. 'You have not served your purpose yet.'

I try to imagine what he might do, and fail.

'You, thrall, are a thief. Nothing more than a slave boy, an ungrateful wretch, hastening his trip to hell by committing such grievous sins. Betrayal. Lies. Thievery. These are the works of coward. You have proven yourself A COWARD.'

From the corner of my eye, I notice Jarl Magnus shifting uncomfortably. *I hope he remembers the rope I threw him across the sea. I may have let him down today, but it wasn't always thus.*

Ljotolf paces before me and his audience. 'As befitting of the fine company we are keeping here—'

'Skál,' interrupts Sven Asleifsson, slamming a horn of ale onto the table so hard the liquid sloshes out over both sides. He wipes his beard of the froth. 'Skál' echo his men as one.

Lord Ljotolf smiles, showing too many of his rotting teeth. 'As I was saying, befitting of the fine company we are keeping here, let's be civilised, shall we? We'll play a game. I'm sure the Archbishop will agree to a little sport. Divine justice will be done, you see? The Almighty can perform a miracle to spare you, boy, or he can let things take their proper course, and you die. We, at least, are going to be diverted.' There is power and fury in his eyes, though he keeps baring his teeth in a smile.

Our own oarsmen stay silent as Sven Asleifsson's warriors, and those of Lord Ljotolf, start banging their fists on the tables and begin chanting for my blood.

Ljotolf spreads his arms wide. 'You against me. Thrall against Lord. Boy against warrior. You lose; you die. It's simple.'

I wonder how long I can bear the tension, the intense gaze of everyone in the room. I take a breath. 'What if I win?'

A whisper of surprise spreads along the benches.

Ljotolf raises his tousled eyebrows. 'Never fear! You won't. But if you do, I'll grant you your freedom. I'm even going to throw in the Archbishop's figures in this sack! Hope you don't mind, Archbishop.' Ljotolf slaps the man of God on the back so hard that he coughs, resulting in more laughter from the crowd. There is a battle building in this drinking hall, just ready to erupt. I can feel it.

'What is the game?' I ask in as clear a voice I can muster.

'Hmm,' muses Ljotolf, looking around at his men for approval. 'A swordfight would be over too quickly, and it's too dark for a race, or arm wrestling. No, none of those things. I was thinking…'

His eyes drift to the bag on the Archbishop's lap. 'Let's have a game of chess. Let's see these precious figures everyone is talking about. Archbishop!'

It's as if the ground shakes. My whole body quivers. The others misinterpret it for fear, but it is hope. Nothing but a little hope, a shred, a skelf, but it's enough.

The man of God wants to protest; I can see it. He doesn't want an oaf like Ljotolf to touch his prized gifts. But he can't argue.

Magnus knows it and feigns disinterest. 'The boy is nothing but a thrall, and a traitor too. He means nothing to me. But would it not be a waste of everyone's time to watch him play like this? He can't possibly know the rules. Lock him up and decide what to do with him at your leisure. I care not!' But his eyes don't match the relaxed tone of his voice. His brain is working—on a plan to rescue me or a plan to kill me, I don't know which.

Lord Ljotolf snaps his fingers in the direction of some women gathered behind him with his lady wife, a plump woman with unremarkable features. 'Bring me a chess board from my chambers. A gaming board, do you hear?'

Hurried steps leave the hall, but I focus on breathing in and out. Death I was expecting, but not this. Not a duel of this kind. How well-practised is Ljotolf in this noble game?

Will the Almighty extend a hand of mercy to the sinner? I have to believe God cares for such as me.

Breathe in and breathe out. The servant woman is back and approaches from behind to unfold a small table. Then she slides a chequered game board onto it. Her hair hangs in red and grey curls over her face and down her shoulders.

I breathe no more.

Because as she withdraws and nods to Lord Ljotolf, she turns, and I am looking straight into the eyes of my mother.

29

THE CHESSMEN TEST

All the men are crowding round the table, but the earth shakes in my blood. Has she even recognised me? How could she? I have grown so much in the years she has been gone, and even before that I barely saw her, living in the workshop. But she is shaken—I can tell. Maybe the look of me stirs something in her heart and I remind her of the child she left behind.

Ljotolf motions for silence. 'It is decided. Friends! Norsemen! Before we eat, let's have some sport with our little runaway—the thrall who dared touch the great treasure belonging to the holy Archbishop of Nidaros himself.'

I can't tell if he is mocking the bishop or not. Jarl Magnus's face is unreadable, but Sven Asleifsson's twitches with malice.

Lord Ljotolf fake-bows a little. 'Before I face my worthy opponent…' I hear more chuckles. 'I wish to know his name, if he has one. So, honoured opponent, what do they call you? Just so I can carve it into the long list of foes who have met their match in Ljotolf of the Isle of Lewis.'

Some of his men are guffawing. I cannot see my mother anymore. If she is still in the room, now is my chance to put it beyond doubt. My throat is rougher than a cat's tongue, but I summon a shred of dignity from somewhere and answer. 'My name is Kylan of Lewis, after the island of my parents. Raised as a thrall in Trondheim, Lord Ljotolf, and at your service. I choose to accept your challenge.'

There is a moment of utter silence at my insolence, and from where the women are standing, there is a sharp gasp. I turn to see my mother being steadied by the servant girl beside her. I catch her eye once more, shimmering with fear and loss the way it did on the day she left. I don't know how I do it, but I manage a smile in her direction.

Lord Ljotolf has recovered as his men begin to mumble again. 'Choose to accept? Ha! You never had a choice, boy. Very well. Let's play.'

His assistant pulls one of the velvet pouches from the leather bag and arranges the figures. I am given the crimson ones, of course. It gives Lord Ljotolf the first move. No matter. Withdrawing into my mind, I try to recall everything that Ingirid taught me. She often said, in our little gaming sessions, that she could outplay and outmanoeuvre most men she knew. I considered it bragging at the time.

I reckon now is when we put her claim to the test.

Lord Ljotolf pulls his first pawn forward and I have no option but to respond. I take care to act uncertain, pretending to be unsure about what moves are permitted or not, just to lull him into a false confidence. I must summon all my concentration if I am to emerge from this maze of turns and counter-turns.

There is a collective gasp, followed by uneasy muttering: I have taken the first of the Lord Ljotolf's pawns. A quick glance over my shoulder confirms that most of the bystanders are astounded that I am able to play at all. Much of the talk centres on the figures themselves, commenting on their beauty and extraordinary craftmanship. In any other situation, I would have revelled in such praise. But my brain is consumed with one thing only: survival. I do not particularly think about attacking Ljotolf's king or capturing his queen. No, my sole aim is to stop him from capturing mine. Soon the chequerboard is covered by an unholy mess of crimson and white, and my head swims. *When did I last sleep?*

Some of the bystanders have wandered away. Perhaps they do not understand the rules and have lost interest. My opponent, however, sits glaring at the board.

'You play well.' It is the voice of Jarl Magnus who has not shifted from his position.

'Thank you,' rasps Ljotolf, but a quick peep up confirms that Jarl Magnus was talking to me.

And that is all it takes, one moment of distraction. 'Ha!' exclaims the island Lord as he captures my queen. I failed to see the threat of his warder and have paid for it dearly. A wave of nausea sweeps through me and my eyes suddenly feel so heavy, that an army of men would struggle to hold them up. There is whimpering from the women's corner. My mother cannot know what is happening on the board, but she will read the men's faces. I raise my eyebrows and nod slowly before willing my lips to curl up. *Act your part; it is your only hope.*

'What?' My opponent is irritated.

'Nothing, noble Lord Ljotolf.'

'You're not distressed?'

'It was part of a plan, my Lord. Soon, your king will be in danger.'

'Impossible!' He is sweating, aware of the fact that his men, his friends and perhaps even enemies are watching, waiting for him to fail.

He is unsettled enough to make a rushed movement with his knight who is swiftly claimed by my pawn. Outraged, he moves his queen forward and I could have sung. My own bishop was waiting in the corner, just willing him to fall into this very trap.

With a flick of the wrist, I replace his queen with my bishop and utter the word, quietly enough to sound humble, but loud enough to be heard.

'Check, sir.'

30

THE LAST MOVE

Sven Asleifsson's may have risen, but I will not yield. I must press my advantage, however much the man with the scars would frighten me. With an effort, I relax my muscles, leaning back as if my life did not depend on the next few minutes. In my mind, I conjure up what will happen next.

He will move his warder across to protect his king.

I will move my bishop to attack the warder, and that will leave the way free for my knight to threaten his king.

He will move his king out of danger, and I will take his warder with my bishop. There is nothing he can do about it.

He behaves just as I expected him to. Jarl Magnus has disappeared for the moment and the Archbishop has withdrawn into a corner of the feasting hall. The air is thick with threat. My knight moves forward, protected by pawns. 'Check,' I whisper again. He says nothing.

'I am fearful, Lord Ljotolf,' I begin again. My voice is stronger now. 'Will you act with honour? Will you keep your promise, should you fail?'

'Be quiet,' he growls. 'You're trying to distract me from my next move.'

I sink into silence once more, biding my time. He acts as I had hoped, sacrificing another pawn, and it suddenly occurs to me that winning may be as dangerous as losing. Sven Asleifsson beside him polishes the side of his sword with his sleeve, caressing it as if its services will soon be required. I swallow hard.

Do I let the island Lord win and then beg for his mercy?

I scrutinise his face carefully, grown round on the butter and cream of his riches. His eyes, grey and unforgiving, seal my choice. He will not show mercy. Despite his chapel beneath the feasting hall, this is not a praying man. He cannot be trusted.

Determination builds in me. I allow him to take a pawn which is met by half-hearted applause from his men. All part of my strategy, but I still make a show of tearing my hair and groaning loudly. There is a tremor in my hand, part intentional as I pretend to be terrified to death, and part real as I steel myself for what is to come.

To lure him towards my side of the board, I place a bait he cannot resist: my bishop, staring out from its ivory isolation, free on the board to tempt him to his downfall. And it works; oh my, how it works! Lord Ljotolf turns around to his men and flashes a wide, brown smile towards Sven Asleifsson. 'Ha, I'll say that for the boy, he gave me a game, did he not? But this oversight will cost him dearly!' He reaches for his warder and slides it across to take my bishop. '*Hark*, Archbishop! Look, I'm doing away with one of your churchmen on the board. I must say, I am much taken with this set. I wish you were going to gift it to me.'

'Then keep it, in exchange for your kind hospitality. You're welcome to it.' There is an edge to the Archbishop's voice now and I wonder that even the patience of such a man of God should have limits. Jarl Magnus has reappeared beside him and whispers. The bishop does not look at me at all during this exchange. I am a lost cause. Outside, the shearwaters fly over the island of my forebears and scream their outrage into the sky. *God Almighty, give me strength for what I am about to do.*

My remaining knight skips over his pawn to take its position and I know I have one shot at this. I must not fail.

'Checkmate,' I croak, loudly enough for all to hear. If the Lord Ljotolf breaks his promise to a twelve-year-old slave boy, these men shall know it.

There is silence as Lord Ljotolf stares at the board, his eyes darting from crimson to white figure, from black to white chequer space. His mouth drops as he assesses his game options and realises in turn that I have pre-empted them all.

His forehead contracts and brews a storm, as I feared it would, and now I cannot take my eyes off him. I have played the game and won. Whatever happens next will not be my doing.

A hound in the corner scratches behind its ears with its hind leg. I only notice because it is the only sound. All eyes are on the island Lord who seems to be fighting a battle with his own rage.

But it is Sven Asleifsson who reacts first. Slowly, he rises, draws his sword and swings it towards my neck with a roar.

31

MOONSTRUCK

The blow I expected does not come. Instead, it is met by another blade! Rolling myself under the table, I catch sight of Sven Asleifsson towering over me. Crossing swords with him is… Jarl Magnus! The Jarl grits his teeth in the effort to push Asleifsson back as I watch open mouthed. Vaguely, in the dank air of the feasting hall, I become aware of other drawn swords, but apart from the two leaders, no one is engaging. Asleifsson heaves and is pushed back, crashing sideways into Lord Ljotolf's seat and suddenly everyone is on their feet. Blade meets blade. Fist meets skin, blood meets bone. There is shoving and yelling and stamping and beating. I feel myself grabbed and yanked up by the scruff of my neck. 'What are you waiting for, boy? To the ship!'

Instinctively I twist round to where the women were seated earlier in the evening, but to be honest I have trouble remembering where the door is at all, or where is up and down. Jarl Magnus doesn't dither but pulls me along, dragging me into the cold night air as the fight continues inside. 'Hither!' he yells, directing our men sideways. 'The Archbishop is already waiting—our ship lies ready in the bay. South, to Somerled!'

The Jarl might have sent someone, or maybe he did it himself when he vanished earlier on. Looking at the stars, I get my bearings at last. There is screaming inside, and hollering. All of a sudden, my weary mind does its job and I remember! I dig my heels into the sand as we approach the waterline.

The Jarl is nearly knocked off balance by my sudden resistance and spins round. 'To the ship!'

More and more of our men run past us to the galley.

'I can't, sir. My mother is in the hall.'

'What?'

There is genuine shock in his face. And something else too.

'I can't abandon my mother, sir. She was taken from me once when I was young. I set out on this journey because I knew she was gone to Lewis. I need to… I can't leave her.'

'Say no more.'

Magnus takes a deep breath and loosens the chains of the ship just as the final two oarsmen climb aboard. He raises his hand, in apology or farewell, to the Archbishop.

The man of God looks helplessly over the side as the

ship is drawn out into the tide. Counting the heads of the rowers, there must be four, maybe five of our men who did not return and the Archbishop himself has taken to the oars.

'But sir, aren't you—'

'Quiet, boy!'

As our ship's sail fills with the night breeze, Ljotolf, Sven and their men pour onto the shore. Some splash into the water after the escaping bishop's party, some throw missiles and stones after them.

No one looks back at the boy and the man who tiptoe in the shadows, making their way back to the entrance of the drinking hall. *We are mad. Absolutely moonstruck. No one, no one could possibly be berserk enough to re-enter the hall, through the only way in and out.*

Some of the injured lie still on the ground, others whimper. I scan the torchlit building for her hair—and it is what leads me to her. Clutching her leg, she rocks backwards and forwards next to the big fireplace, her face buried in her bloodstained garment. Another servant girl is moving between the injured attempting to see to their wounds.

Jarl Magnus follows me, sword drawn.

'There. That's her,' I point.

Stepping towards her, I place a hand on her shoulder. 'Mother!'

She raises her head, but keeps her eyes closed. 'Don't

toy with me. I cannot bear it.' Her face is ash-stained and crusted with tears. There is a scratch across her cheek, but it does not look serious. Her leg is another matter. There is a slash—she must have been caught in the cross-fighting.

My low voice becomes more urgent. 'Mother, it really is me. Open your eyes! I've returned but if we are to leave together, we must leave NOW, do you hear?' She opens her eyes a chink and suddenly clutches me with both hands, clawing into my side. I embrace her just as hard. 'Can you walk, Mother?'

She shakes her head in anguish. 'No. But go. Go, Kylan, go! Please, you must…' At this point she sees Jarl Magnus, with his weapon and stifles a cry.

'Don't worry, Mother, this is a good man. He's been like a father to me and is risking his life even now to protect me.'

'No time to explain.' Jarl Magnus has had enough and simply scoops Mother's slight figure up. I pick up a sword from the stone floor and head in front of them, but something catches my eye. *The bag! The leather bag with the remaining chessmen.* Four more sets will be in it, if I remember right. I reach for it and go—the Archbishop's treasure does not belong in the hands of Lord Ljotolf, or of Sven Asleifsson. I sling the bag over my shoulder. Magnus makes a warning gesture. The most dangerous moment is still to come: passing through the narrow exit back out into the night where Ljotolf and Sven Asleifsson are baying for our blood.

We approach the doorway like a stag approaches a stream, hearing the wolves howl.

On the shore, the Orkneymen and the Lewismen weave in and out of each other to reach their own ships. One is already being pushed out to sea to make after the Archbishop and our crew, but it doesn't get far. We hear the cursing and raging even from here. Jarl Magnus shrugs. 'I holed their ships, earlier in the evening. I could see how the night would turn out,' he whispers in my ear.

My mother shivers, touching the congealed blood on her shin.

Of course! Her knowledge of this place may yet get us out of here.

The Jarl seems to be thinking the same. 'What's your name, woman?' he asks in a soft voice. My mother's eyes are rolling back.

'Her name is Hilda. Hilda.' I lean in closely and rub her shoulder. 'Mother, we need your help. Don't give up. I'm here. Kylan, your boy. I'm really here. Not a dream.'

'Hush!' snaps Jarl Magnus.

We linger at the building's corner as seven or eight of Asleifsson's men run back towards the shore, gesticulating to their leader. No doubt they have discovered that their own ships are holed through, too.

Once they are clear of us, Jarl Magnus tries again. 'Hilda. Hilda! We need your help. Where does Ljotolf keep his fishing boats? We need a small vessel, but seaworthy.'

At first, I think that my mother will not answer at all, and Magnus gives her a frustrated shake. I glare at him. Then I notice. 'Sir! Her hand, look. She is pointing.'

He hesitates. 'Is she even conscious?'

We follow the direction of her outreached fingers, up the hillside. Once we round the top, painfully aware of our silhouettes outlined by the lightening sky in the east, we see them—two vessels by a workshop. One looks brand-new.

'Is she seaworthy yet?' I frown.

'Only one way to find out!'

Jarl Magnus tips my mother into the upturned boat. 'Are you going to help me or not?'

'Sorry!'

I pull with all my might.

The truth is, I have a feeling.

And it isn't good.

32

THE BERSERKER

The boat would be heavy enough for a man and a boy, but with a full-grown woman inside, it is almost impossible.

A mere knife's throw is all the distance we seek to travel. But it may as well be the furthest corner of the world. We push and pull, all the while watching the lightening horizon. *Quick, quick. The cover of night is our best bet.* Frantic efforts to repair the holed ships seem to be underway while messengers run from the residence's armoury with armfuls of swords. I can see the round outlines of the men's shields as they stand lined up in the distance.

Wait! The same must be true in reverse. If I can see them…

'Down!'

Footsteps are rounding the corner, and Jarl Magnus manages to flip the boat around only just in time, tipping my mother's limp shape onto the ground and hiding both of us under the vessel with her. We are plunged into darkness, with sea kelp and fear saturating me from the toes up. Surely, whoever is passing by will realise that this boat does not belong here. But then the most unwelcome words are uttered, right beside our upturned hiding place. 'Call the Lord Ljotolf. We can take these small boats and give chase. This one here is already halfway to the water.'

Running steps fade into the distance.

With soundless breath, I peer through the gap between the boat's rim and the sand. I can see two pairs of feet. One of the men appears to be leaning onto our boat. *Of course. They will be just as weary as we are.* I feel around behind me. Mother is not stirring, but the Jarl is crouching near me. I find his hand with mine and press two fingers down into his palm twice, firmly. Two. Two men.

I feel him creeping forward and the bristles of his beard on my ear. 'Now, Kylan. Before the others get here.'

'NOW!' He repeats with a shout and I use all my shoulder strength to push the boat off us, knocking the leaning man into the sand where he scrambles away from us on his back, thrashing. His companion has launched himself at Jarl Magnus's neck, clawing into his face, preventing him from reaching his dropped sword. I pick it up and bring it down into the man's calf. He collapses with a yelp.

Jarl Magnus shakes his head, rubs his neck and immediately points over my shoulder. There must be seventy or eighty warriors running at us: shields, swords, spears, all noise and clamour. Lord Ljotolf is near the front, his eyes alive with rage.

Just ahead of him is Sven Asleifsson, foaming at the mouth, beating and biting his shield like the chess figure I saw Gunnar carve so long ago. Even from here I can see the red-flecked whites of his eyes.

Jarl Magnus and I spring into action in the same heartbeat.

'He's gone berserk! BERSERK! Boy, I've seen this before. TO SEA!'

The Jarl takes the boat by himself and I hook my elbows under my mother's arms and drag her towards the water with the bag of chessmen bashing into my knees. I have to run backwards, meaning I can see how quickly the enemies are gaining on us, especially Sven who seems to be propelled forward by the Devil himself.

Twice I nearly fall, but then I feel the sea seep into my shoes. The boat is afloat, but only just. I wade in, and Magnus drags my mother into the vessel. I clamber after them; desperation lends me speed and strength in equal measure. Once in, I struggle to my feet to see.

Magnus has used his long sword to push off and we stoop as three axes fly overhead. More worryingly, one weapon embeds itself in the side of the boat as a large wave sweeps us out to sea. I reach over to pull it out, but Magnus reprimands me sharply. 'LEAVE it!' he yells. 'It plugs the hole it created, for now at least. If you pull it out, we'll sink for sure.'

Just then, the boat gives a violent jolt.

A hand clamps onto the side of the boat. Then another. With a second gigantic jolt, which nearly unseats me and causes my mother to slide to the furthest edge of the vessel, the hulking shape of Sven Asleifsson hauls himself into the boat, muscles rippling and dripping with seawater. The boat is barely bigger than a saint's coracle. Sven breathes heavily, pulling his broadsword from his belt.

The Jarl is ready. Like a cat, he springs up too, his legs wide to keep stable. Asleifsson swings his sword for my head and I duck, crawling to the corner to protect my mother. In the morning dawn, sparks fly above us as metal meets metal once more. The waves are picking up, but the two warring men are matched in skill, weight and balance. The difference is, Asleifsson is barely a man at all but a predator, a starving bear. He wants blood and does not mind where it comes from. I throw myself into him from the side, but it has no more impact than rocking the boat sideways. Both men have anticipated it and shift their weight from foot to foot like true Viking seafarers. Asleifsson parries a blow from the Jarl and bends sideways, causing my friend to lose his balance. Sven takes advantage, ramming his sword towards Magnus's chest. The Jarl only just manages to raise his sword in time but lacks the strength to push back. Asleifsson's blade runs off the sword and pierces Magnus's shoulder, tearing into his upper arm too. Asleifsson roars his victory as Magnus collapses into the boat.

I have no weapon! The villain raises his and I confess my sins in that split second, my face pressed into the stolen bag of chess pieces. Asleifsson's blade slashes towards my neck.

I don't know how it happens, but instinctively, my body convulses sideways and Asleifsson misses. I launch my arms over the rim of the boat. With both hands, I grab the hilt of the axe still embedded there, wrench it out and swing the blunt end before he can react, bringing it down onto the back of his knees. The giant teeters at the edge of the boat for a brief moment. It's as if the seabirds stop shrieking, the wind stops howling, the waves stop crashing, only for a breath. Like a stuffed doll, Asleifsson topples backwards from our boat and is swallowed by the waves. Moments later, he resurfaces a couple of horses' lengths away. Without thinking, I stumble towards the bench of the boat and use the axe to hew out the plank of wood.

'Here!'

I throw it to the villain who curses and makes for the

shore again, kicking his legs as I ram the axe back into its hole on the side of the boat to secure it.

Asleiffson's fate is in the hands of the Almighty now. But mine—mine I can do something about. I take the oar which is still in its hook and begin, paddling left and right and left and right. When I am absolutely certain that the tide will not carry us back where we have just fled, I allow myself a rest and a prayer.

By the time I bind up Mother's and Jarl Magnus's wounds with strips of my tunic, we have rounded a large expanse of sandy bay and the tip of the island. Just to be sure, I row a little further. The leather bag of chessmen containing its four velvet pouches accuses me from where it lies.

The clouds are building.

The waves are rising.

And the dagger of a guilty conscience pierces my heart.

33

REDEMPTION

At long last, daylight arrives. Seen from the shore, our boat must look like a fleck of brown dirt, spoiling the glossy surface of the sea. Approaching the headland, the rocks and the waves toss it like a thrush tosses a snail. I crouch in the middle, tipping my own weight this way and that to keep the vessel balanced. My right arm is stretched towards the rudder, such as it is, in the face of the power of these waves.

But I believe in a greater power still and my left arm curls tighter around the leather bag, so tight in fact that my knuckles show white against my ruddy skin. If I can reach land, I will do as I must. I will save my soul. Even if it means losing my life in the saving.

The rocks are near, so near, and I squint against the salt-spray, forcing myself to breathe. Above me, the clouds churn, solid enough to swallow up earth and sea. And me with it.

Can there be a more remote, godforsaken place than this?

No?

Good.

I ride the wave as it carries the boat towards the coast. I have done my best with the bandages to my mother's leg and Magnus's shoulder. But both need fresh water, as do I.

I try to use the momentum of the tide to haul the boat to shore, ramming an oar into the sand and securing it further with a rope. I won't be long. I can't be long.

Tired steps sink into the pristine sand. A building lies ahead. A ruin.

As I approach there is a rustling, and a barn owl flies from the crumbling window with quiet wingbeats while its young call from their nest inside. I take it as a good omen. Walking around the old stone walls, I listen. The tinkle of a stream. God be praised!

I drop the bag and close my eyes. *Guide me, Lord.* I feel my feet press forward, around the ruin where a half-sand-buried wooden stair leads to what can only have been an underground storage room.

Here.

I feel it, powerfully.

Here.

I sense my eyes filling with tears. These chessmen, carved at my workshop all the way back in Trondheim, have been my constant companions all these days. But they are not mine, as much as I would wish it.

God, have mercy on me. The prayer is on my lips as I retreat from the corner where I have buried them. Ljotolf still has the set we played with. No doubt, when Ljotolf is overthrown by another, the gaming pieces will be owned by that man, and his sons and grandsons after him. But these figures here, hidden in the sand may never be found again—may never be seen again, played with again.

Something tugs at my soul and I wish that one day, others will marvel at their beauty. But I dismiss the urge to dig them out once more. *What will be will be.* The Almighty will see to it. I, on the other hand, have a task. Stumbling up the hillside, I take the leather bag which held the figures and fill it to the tip with fresh, peaty Lewis water. The waters of home.

Drinking first, Jarl Magnus inspects the bandage and grimaces with the pain. 'I have been fortunate indeed,' he concedes. 'It is not so very deep.' He looks up at me. 'Why didn't you run him through? You had the chance to split his skull.'

I nod thoughtfully. 'The Almighty did not make me a killer.' I say it without regret. 'There are blue flowers and white; there are different kinds of deer, and dogs, and men. The Lord did not make me a Viking.'

The Jarl nods slowly and passes the water bag to my

mother whose wound is beginning to crust up. I have washed it again in fresh water and it may yet heal. The slumber has done her good. Her head is resting on the Jarl's uninjured shoulder, but he does not seem to mind. With relief, I push the boat back into the surf. *I have done right. For once, I am certain of that.*

If I can round the headland and push on to the isle they call Harris, Jarl Magnus says, there is a new and powerful Lord, the Gael called Somerled. He has a hold on those Southern Isles and may grant us land after the old Viking law. The Jarl seemed hopeful. 'I can wield a sword and I know the ways of the seas. He may accept my service.'

And with that, I allow the waves control of my life again and watch the secret resting place of the chessmen, until the clouds and waves brush it out completely. Turning my face south to Harris, I row, watching my own muscles flex and ripple.

Perhaps in all of this, I have become a man.

EPILOGUE

THE LAST THROW OF THE KNIFE

Magnus stands tall on the stretch of land the Lord Somerled of the Isles has offered us in his mercy. Mother beside him wraps the shawl tighter around herself and rests her head on his shoulder before stepping aside for prayer. It's still odd, the way that the two of them suffered alongside each other that night and then healed alongside each other at the Harris farmstead. We were given shelter there, in exchange for my labour as a skilled craftsman. Old Erik's tools are my most treasured possession now. I toiled while their wounds closed—and where they healed each other's inner scars too, the scars of the mind. The scars of memory.

Magnus talked then, about his demons. The images that haunt him of the Crusades, the things he was forced to do in the name of our Lord. The things his bishops urged him to do, just as his conscience forbade it. They crush him even now, his own deeds, and the deeds of others which he did nothing to prevent.

And then he speaks of his own mother who begged the young man not to desert her and join the Crusaders. The mother who died alone in his absence, unfed and undefended. No wonder my words stirred something in him. *I cannot leave her.*

My mother, in turn, has someone to look after her and to protect her.

The witnesses at the side of the field nod. Magnus raises his knife and throws. It whistles through the air and embeds itself in a clump of moss just by the cliffside. Appreciative murmurs rise from the crowd. He has strength, that man, despite the scars and the lines splitting his forehead. I run to retrieve the weapon, driving a stick into the ground where the blade struck, and jog back to hand it to him. He turns, pulls back his arm and hurls it as far as he can in the opposite direction, up the hillside where it bounces off a rock and lies still. I drive a stick in there too.

Another throw, this time east where the sun rises. It's a particularly powerful throw. It takes me some time to find the knife, driven hard into the ground, and when I wave back the assembled crowd cheers loudly. I love the tradition of our forebears, granting land as far as a man could throw a knife. All we have to do is build a fence by the time a year is out, and it is ours, granted in exchange for our labour and our service, should war come to these lands. It seems like a fair bargain to me.

This time when I return the knife, the blade is a little bent, but Magnus laughs anyway. Sunset. The knife must fly to chase the sun at the final throw. I expect him to throw straight away, but he hesitates. Glancing around at Mother, I can see she wonders why, too. He is doing battle within himself, wrestling with something. But then an expression of determination claims victory over his features.

'Kylan! Come here a moment.'

I obey. Is his shoulder still ailing him? Have I displeased him?

I expected words, or instructions perhaps. Instead, he holds out his hand, the bent knife balanced on his palm.

I inhale deeply. *Our homestead. Magnus, Mother and I. For now, and for the future.*

I try not to overthink it. Stepping forward, I square up to the setting sun, raise the knife and hurl it west with all my might. It paints a perfect arc, riding the wind, surfing the sunrays and finally burying itself in the earth, barely still within sight. There is silence.

But only for a moment. The bystanders burst into claps and cheers and I feel myself swept into the air as Magnus lifts me onto his good shoulder, giving a dance of relief and triumph. Our homestead will have land. Much land, good land.

Mother crashes into us with a hug and we collapse in

a heap, brushing our faces clear of grass and moss before rolling over and breathing deeply. Overhead, gulls shriek with joy and the heavens answer with fire. Can Ingirid see this same sky? Can Old Erik? Can Freya?

In the clouds, moving darkly above, I fancy I can see chessmen shapes, swords, ships and shields, but they soon dissolve into nothing but wisps, nothing but light brushstrokes on this glorious parchment.

For the first time in my life, I am home.

THE END

GLOSSARY

Ale—a type of beer
Apothecaries—people who prepared/ sold medicines
Archbishop—a bishop of the highest rank, who is in charge of all the churches across a region
Asgard—the home of the gods in Norse mythology
Berserker—a furiously violent fighter who is out of control
Breeches—trousers
Broch—a tall iron-age roundhouse
Bu—Earl's residence which has a large drinking hall
Casket—box
Chapel—small church
Checkmate—a chess player says this when the opponent has no more options and is defeated
Confession—when you tell your sins/wrongs to God
Cope—a bishop's cloak
Coracle—a small, round, lightweight boat
Crimson—a deep, dark red
Crozier—a hooked staff carried by a bishop
Crusade—violent medieval wars to conquer the lands where the bible is set for Christians
Diocese—a church district
Drinking horn—the hollowed out horn of a cow or goat, used as a drinking vessel
Evensong—evening church worship
Forebears—ancestors
Gaelic—language spoken in Scotland at the time
Galley—a long ship propelled by rowing. (see ***Longship***)

Gargoyle—stone carving of grotesque creature
Hacksilver—silver loot hacked to pieces and weighed. Viking currency
Heilir—Norse Greeting plural
Heill—Norse greeting singular
Hnefatafl—a simpler boardgame, popular in Viking times and similar to chess
Holy Land—modern day Israel and Palestine, setting of the bible
Ivory—a hard, white material from animal tusks
Jarl—a Norse chief
Karl—free man in Norse society
Kraken—a legendary gigantic sea-monster
Loki—Norse god of mischief
Longship—a sail-and-oar type of galley; Viking warship
Medici—medieval doctors
Mitre—a bishop's and archbishop's traditional hat
Nidaros—the medieval name of Trondheim
Norse—early medieval Scandinavian society and language
Northern Isles—Orkney and Shetland, referred to as *Norðreyjar* in Old Norse
Odin—Norse God of war and king of Asgard
Overcoat—woollen outer garment
Pawn—chess figure of smallest size and value
Rune—Norse letter symbols
Saga—heroic story
Sanctuary—a holy space that offers protection
Saxony—now Northwest Germany

Scabbard—protective covering for a sword
Scholar—educated person or one who attends school
Scotus—someone from Scotland
Shearwaters—seabirds
Skál—a drinking expression, like *cheers*
Skald—poet or storyteller
Skiff—a light rowing boat
Southern Isles—The Hebrides and the Isle of Man, called *Suðreyjar* in Old Norse
Stern—the back of a ship
Stoorworm—huge and evil mythical sea-serpent
Thor—hammer-wielding Norse god associated with lightning, thunder and strength.
Thrall—slave in Viking society
Tillerman—the sailor who steers the ship using a tiller
Trondheim—city in Norway, likely place of origin for the Lewis Chesspieces
Tusk—long pointed tooth
Valhalla—Odin's great hall where slain warriors go after death
Vespers—early evening prayer
Voilà—French exclamation meaning *there it is!*
Warder—medieval chess piece (today's rook)

A LITTLE BIT ABOUT THE LEWIS CHESSMEN

The famous Lewis Chessmen belong to a hoard of almost a hundred 12th century gaming pieces which were discovered in the parish of Uig on the Isle of Lewis in 1831.

They are carved from walrus ivory, with a handful likely made from whale's teeth. No one knows exactly when or where they were crafted, but experts have worked out that the figures belong to several chess sets and were made by around five craftsmen of varying skill, each with a unique style. Most scholars agree that the figures were most likely carved in Trondheim, although a minority have suggested they could also be the work of the famous Icelandic carver Margrét hin haga. Records place her slightly later, but I loved the idea of a famous woman carver so much that I added her in anyway.

The church was very powerful in the early Middle Ages. A new Archdiocese, a kind of church government, was established in Trondheim (then called Nidaros) in the 1150s. This coincided with records of the Orkney Earl's Crusade. It made sense for a new Archbishop to visit the places under his rule, and to bring gifts. Orkney and the Hebrides were still largely occupied by Norsemen. It is unusual that the chess pieces include warriors and bishops, as well as, for the first time, the female figure of the Queen.

Many of the characters really existed, although not all records are equally reliable: Jon Birgersson, Earl Ragnvald Kali Kolsson, Ingirid and her son Elin, Sven Asleifsson (sometimes spelled Asleifarson), Ljotolf and Somerled for example. In my imagination, the chess pieces which Ljotolf and Kylan play with in the book are later claimed by the Gaelic leader Somerled. Around a century afterwards, a praise poem refers to Somerled's great-grandson Aonghas inheriting his '*brown ivory chess sets.*'

The chess pieces are now on public display. You can see them in the British Museum in London where they have been declared one of the top ten treasures of our nation, or in the National Museum of Scotland. A small number can be found at the Museum nan Eilean in Stornoway on the Isle of Lewis. All of them are beautiful; perhaps more so because of the mysteries which surround them.

There is much we do not know. However, one thing is certain: these Viking treasures and their secrets will fascinate young and old for generations to come.

ACKNOWLEDGEMENTS

I owe a huge debt of gratitude to all the people who have made *The Chessmen Thief* possible and I feel blessed beyond all measure. I thank God for you all as this story begins to navigate the chequered board of the book world.

THE KING: My father Wolfgang Haas who taught me chess and kept me intrigued with the game, while really just toying with me. I never became a great chess player, but I have retained a life-long love of the game, largely because of my love for him. I miss him.

THE QUEEN: Anne Glennie, my publisher, editor, cover designer, typesetter, all round champion, agony aunt and friend. Just like a chess queen, there is basically nothing that woman can't do! Her enthusiasm for the project gave me courage to move forward from the very start. If the queen had an understudy, she would be called Sandra McGowan, my wonderful friend who has once more wielded her magic to bring the book to life in her gorgeous illustrations.

THE ROOKS: My family are the castle that keeps me safe, wherever the game takes me. Thank you to Rob, Carla, Isla and Duncan for always, always having my back. Thanks too, to my mother Ursula Haas and my sisters Ricarda and Margund for their encouragement, and for hunting around for old chess photos so that I could reminisce.

THE KNIGHTS: Thank you to all those battling their way through the book world alongside me—my fellow Clan Cranachan authors, my SCBWI tribe, the Inverness children's writers and all my pals and champions who encourage and cheer me on. The route forward is never straightforward, but we'll get there!

THE BISHOPS: Many thanks to the two learned ones who offered invaluable advice on plotting, both called David. Chief of these is Dr David Caldwell, President of the Society of Antiquaries and former Keeper of Scotland and Europe at the National Museum of Scotland. He gave me early feedback on my plot, and the book he co-edited, *The Lewis Chessmen: New Perspectives*, has been my constant companion. Also thanks to Professor David Worthington who pointed out the next logical moves more than once.

THE PAWNS: Special thanks to our friends Andrew and Cathy Golder for accompanying Rob and I to beautiful (and very stormy) Orkney so that I could research the lie of the land. This book is but one happy by-product of that friendship. I also want to thank my book-penpals at Comely Park Primary School, Crossford Primary School, St Joseph's Primary School and my Scottish Book Trust residency school at Findochty for their input into choosing the main character's name.

AUTHOR'S NOTE

Rewind to 2004 when we lived in London for a brief spell. I had a child at nursery, a toddler, and I was pregnant with our third child. My cultural lifeline was the weekly late opening at the British Museum. On many Wednesday nights, as soon as my husband returned from work, I'd set off, walking to Bloomsbury and taking in the treasures of the world. It was there that I first encountered the Lewis Chessmen.

Fast forward to a holiday on the Isle of Lewis, some fifteen years later. I stood in front of a display cabinet at the Museum & Tasglann nan Eilean at Lews Castle. Face to face with the figures, their story began to intrigue me more and more.

I resolved to read about them, visited the small museum at Uig and even made the trip to Edinburgh to see more of the figures in the National Museum of Scotland as soon as I could. I returned from the capital, heavy-laden with one of the most expensive books I have ever purchased: *The Lewis Chessmen: New Perspectives* which opened my eyes to new story possibilities. The burying of the figures at Méalasta, for example, and the competing arguments for the origin of the pieces in Trondheim or Iceland.

What particularly appealed to me was the detail of how the pieces were made—walrus ivory in the main, carved by the skilled hands of possibly four craftsmen, each with their own distinct style.

Viking and Norse culture have long fascinated me. What's not to like? There are moods and feuds, quests and quarrels aplenty. The Orkneyinga Saga became my new obsession, an intoxicating blend of a culture on the cusp. Viking raids continued alongside the newly established church and its Crusades. Scrappy, dangerous and dramatic—exactly how I like my stories.

And into that mix, throw chess—that most structured and disciplined of games. My father was a committed chess player who competed at club and regional level for most of my childhood. Through him, the man who taught me to play, I had a deeply personal connection with the game of chess. I loved it—because I loved him.

Just like they were in my childhood home, it turns out that games were serious business in the Viking world. Viking life was a chessboard of choices, moves, plots and plans. Survival depended on decisions and on daring. *The Chessmen Thief* certainly swept me along in its icy current of events. It is my hope that readers will give themselves over to the tale as gladly as I did.

Let's play.

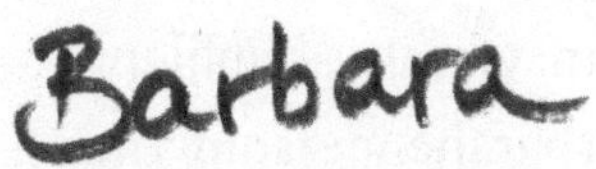

ABOUT THE AUTHOR

Inverness-based Barbara Henderson is the author of historical novels *Fir for Luck*, *Punch*, *Black Water*, *The Siege of Caerlaverock* and *The Chessmen Thief* as well as the eco-thriller *Wilderness Wars.*

Her energetic school visits have taken her across the length and breadth of Scotland, and sometimes beyond. As a Drama teacher, she loves to get young people on their feet as they respond to stories. 'Writing is like magic,' she says. 'I see something in my imagination, and I try to capture it by writing it down—nothing more than black marks on white paper. Much later, young people see these black marks on white paper and suddenly they see something too, feel something of their own. I cannot think of anything more special than that.'

Barbara shares her home with one teenage son, one long-suffering husband and a scruffy Schnauzer called Merry.

Web: barbarahenderson.co.uk
Twitter @scattyscribbler
Instagram: @scattyscribbler
FB: @barbarahendersonwriter

Photo credit: Duncan Henderson